Please return/renew this item by the last date shown on this label, or on your self-service receipt.

To renew this item, visit **www.librarieswest.org.uk** or contact your library.

Your Borrower number and PIN are required.

Libraries**West**

BY THE SAME AUTHOR

Novels

I Too Had a Love Story

Can Love Happen Twice?

Anthology

Love Stories That Touched My Heart (ed.)

Like it Happened Yesterday

RAVINDER SINGH

Penguin
metro reads

PENGUIN METRO READS
Published by the Penguin Group
Penguin Books India Pvt. Ltd, 7th Floor, Infinity Tower C, DLF Cyber City,
Gurgaon 122 002, Haryana, India
Penguin Group (USA) Inc., 375 Hudson Street, New York, New York 10014, USA
Penguin Group (Canada), 90 Eglinton Avenue East, Suite 700, Toronto, Ontario,
M4P 2Y3, Canada
Penguin Books Ltd, 80 Strand, London WC2R 0RL, England
Penguin Ireland, 25 St Stephen's Green, Dublin 2, Ireland (a division of Penguin
Books Ltd)
Penguin Group (Australia), 707 Collins Street, Melbourne, Victoria 3008, Australia
Penguin Group (NZ), 67 Apollo Drive, Rosedale, Auckland 0632, New Zealand
Penguin Books (South Africa) (Pty) Ltd, Block D, Rosebank Office Park, 181 Jan
Smuts Avenue, Parktown North, Johannesburg 2193, South Africa

Penguin Books Ltd, Registered Offices: 80 Strand, London WC2R 0RL, England

First published in Penguin Metro Reads by Penguin Books India 2013

Copyright © Ravinder Singh 2013

All rights reserved

10 9 8 7 6 5 4 3

ISBN 9780143418801

Typeset in Bembo Roman by SÜRYA, New Delhi
Printed at Replika Press Pvt. Ltd, India

A PENGUIN RANDOM HOUSE COMPANY

To my loving parents . . .

Author's Note

Before you start reading my work and before I start narrating my story to you, let me take a minute first and thank you! for choosing to spend your precious hours and days with me. In this busy world, where everyone has a story, a status or a tweet to tell people what's on their mind, your choosing to spend hours reading my story is praiseworthy. And if you are the one who chose not to borrow this novel, but buy, read and keep this personal copy on your bookshelf, then here is my **Thank you again!** to you. You could have spent that money watching a movie in a mall or eating a sandwich with French fries and cola, but you spent that money buying my work and supporting me in continuing to write—which means a lot to me. I have related this story with all my heart and I hope that in my experiences you will find a bit of yourself on every page.

It is interesting for me to recall, when I was a kid and used to go to school, I wanted to be a young man and go to college. And when I did grow into a young man and started going to college, I wanted to get a job and earn my own money. And, now that it has been a decade that I started earning my own money, guess what I wish for?

I now wish I could turn the time around and go back to school again. My life at present is not bad at all. But then there is something . . .

Something that makes me want to run back in time. Something that makes me believe that the then sense of satisfaction in saving my pocket money beats my current happiness of earning my own money. Something that makes me suspect that the expectation to finish my homework was a lot more easier to fulfil than the present expectations of twenty different things at work and at home!

Perhaps this is because, along with all the good things, every passing year of my life has dumped more and more responsibilities on my shoulders. Perhaps it's because, apart from all the happy thoughts in my mind, there are a hundred concerns running in parallel. And all this makes me miss that time of my life when I had a relaxed and carefree mind. When the biggest worry in my life was to score well in the next test.

Childhood days are extremely special. I am sure you too feel the same about your own. But no matter how hard I wish to go back in time, the truth is that I can't do so. And that's why I am writing this book. Because, by doing so, I believe I am going to relive that time of my life—for one more time! Somewhere within the pages of this book, I want to capture those beautiful, innocent, crazy, curiosity-filled and memorable days of my life.

So the story in this book is about those days when mobile phones, the Internet and ATM cards hadn't yet invaded lives. It is of the time when Doordarshan was the only available channel on Indian television sets, and the broadcast of *Ramayan* and *Mahabharat* on Sundays meant less traffic on the road for that one hour. When playing a movie at home meant renting a VCR along with the movie cassette. When having a bicycle of your own was the ultimate goal. It is of the time when it made sense for the shopkeeper and the buyer to return a change of twenty-five paise.

Indeed back then, many of the present world's inventions that have made our lives easier, were yet to be made. But the beauty of those moments is that, even without those inventions, the life then was a lot simpler than what it is today.

Also because I believe, no matter where you go, what you do and what you become, the past remains an important part of your being. It shapes how you think, how you handle situations and how you finally turn out.

As I take you back to that era, my wish for you is that you too go back to your childhood and trace your steps to today with me. I want you to discover your joys, your fears and your tears . . . the way everything happened with you back then. And when you do so, come back and share your childhood memories with me.

Happiness Always,
Ravin

1

First Day, First School

I cried. And I cried hard.

I think I had never cried like that ever before. Till then I didn't need to.

It was my first day in school. I had been admitted to the nursery class.

My father had held my left hand in the warm safety of his right hand. All I did was to keep pleading with him to not leave me alone. Till then, I had never been away from my family. And Dad was trying to do exactly that. I was scared at the very thought of being without Mom, without Dad. It didn't matter for how long—what mattered was that the very next moment there wouldn't be anyone around me whom I knew. Dad was going to leave me among strangers, many of whom were of my age and a few older. The anxiety I suffered was tremendous.

I wanted to talk to Dad and explain to him what it meant for me to be left out of the family this way. But neither did I have the words in my mouth, nor was Dad prepared to listen. And even though I would have known what to say, I wasn't sure how to express what I was feeling. All I could do was cry. So I cried, despite my heavy, wet eyes. I cried despite my leaky nose, and I cried till my throat became hoarse. For some unknown reason, I was hopeful that seeing my terrible condition, Dad would have some mercy on me. That he wouldn't leave me but take me back home, to the soft cocoon—my mother.

But he didn't.

Rather, he left me in that unknown place called 'school', which I began to hate with all my heart in the first hour itself. He handed me to two of the 'ma'ams', who grabbed me by the shoulder and dragged me away with them as I tried my best to run away. For a few minutes, I was hanging from their arms, above the ground, paddling my legs in the air desperately. I bit the hand of the ma'am who had grabbed my shoulder from the left, and succeeded in escaping her grip. I pulled up myself with full energy and slid out of the clasp of the second one as well. Then I ran straight towards Dad, who was about to step out of the classroom.

I wrapped myself tight around his right leg and clutched his white pajama in my hands. In the grip of my front teeth was the corner of his kurta. I was ready to tear it apart but not let it go. But Dad didn't stop. Instead, he began to walk faster so that he could escape my hold.

But the fear of not being able to survive without my family made me cling stronger to him. The louder I cried, the heavier I panted—I had succeeded in creating a scene in front of everyone. And I was absolutely not ashamed of it at all!

It happens—this shameless display of emotions, when you realize your worst fears are about to come true. At that time, I was merely a child. I have seen grown-ups creating a scene too, when faced with their worst fears.

Well, I kept holding on to my father with all my strength, so much so that, when he dragged his leg ahead, my little body got dragged along with him.

'Nahi, Daddy . . . please mainu chadd ke nai jao . . . please, Daddy,' [No, Daddy . . . please don't leave me alone . . . please, Daddy] I wailed loudly in Punjabi.

But it seemed to have quite the opposite effect on him. Being older and stronger, he scolded me in his loud, angry voice and stretched out his palm as if he was going to give me a slap. Then he yanked away my little arms to release himself and handed me back to the teachers, who were more cautious this time about holding me. I saw my father walk away from the classroom. I couldn't do anything.

At that very moment, I hated him.

And now that I hated my father, I loved my mother much more than I ever did. So I started missing her.

I was left sobbing in the class. The sound of my crying lasted as long as it could.

When all my energy had been drained, I became quiet and went to sit in one of the corners of the classroom. I was still scared, but it had been more than an hour, and I suppose I was getting a little used to the environment around me. I also realized that it wasn't just me who was crying. There were plenty of others. And, just like me, they were all in the navy-blue-and-white uniforms. I wondered how come all their parents had ended up choosing the same clothes as my parents had chosen for me. A girl in the far corner was still crying. She had more energy to sustain her agitation than I did. She was also louder than me.

Sitting alone there, I thought to myself—What would I do without my family? I believed that Dad had left me at that place forever. I remembered my mother. I remembered her love for me. I wanted to run into her lap and complain to her about Dad for what he had done to me, that too in front of strangers!

But I didn't even know the way to my home. I wondered if Mom was missing me. Thinking of her my eyes became moist again, not that they had dried out completely. But, this time, I cried quietly. I was much too exhausted to shout any more.

Suddenly, one of the two teachers approached me. She raised my chin with her hand and asked, 'Kya hua, Ravinder? Kyun ro rahe ho?' [What happened, Ravinder? Why are you crying?]

Through a choked nose, I said, 'Hu . . . hu . . . hu . . .

mujhe . . . hu . . . hu . . . mujhe Mommy ke pass jaana hai . . . aaaaaaaaa . . .' [I want to go to my Mommy] and continued to cry.

The teacher wiped my wet, dirty face with the handkerchief that my mother had pinned on to my shirt. She sighed and smiled. Then she promised me that she would take me to my mother. I looked into her eyes. She appeared to be telling the truth, or maybe I didn't have any other choice but to believe her.

'Sacchi?' [Really?] I asked and so many hopes started swimming in my eyes.

'Haan. Lekin tumhe meri baat maanni padegi,' [Yes. But for that you will have to listen to what I say] she offered.

And soon I was game for all that she wanted me to do. I sat where she asked me to sit. I played the games she wanted me to play with the other kids in the class. There were lots of toys and balloons around me, and lots of kids playing with them. In a short while, I had made new friends. I still didn't know their names, but I was happy.

Each one of us, for whom that day marked the first day of school life, had his or her own level of insecurity about each other. But it took only a short while for us to shed our inhibitions. Human nature is strange. Just because we all had a common thing to be afraid of, we turned into friends. In that new and unfamiliar environment, the only support was seeing people who were just like me—and that made things a little comfortable.

In my mind then, I was happy to think that at the end of all this, I would meet my mother and all would be fine. I would tell her about the cruelty of my father and she would never let me go again!

~

Two years passed by in understanding what a school was all about. By the time I got into Class I, I had finally accepted that there was no escaping school. I had a fair idea of what my life was going to look like for the next twelve years, or even more if I failed midway. My friends from the class, too, didn't have any idea about what else to do with their lives; so they accepted what their parents asked them to do. I thought it was safe to follow everyone. And, so, I accepted going to school.

But now that I had accepted going to school, my parents upgraded their level of expectations.

'Study well. You have to come first!'

When I nodded my head to that demand at that time, I never realized that I had stepped on the starting line of what later was going to become a rat race.

2

Happiness in Little Things

Our family lived in Burla, a very small, peaceful town situated beside the river Mahanadi in the western part of the state of Orissa. Hirakud Dam, once known as the world's longest dam, was just four kilometres from the place where I lived. Because of its importance, Hirakud Dam had become a landmark for Burla—a dam which the little, sleepy town was very proud of.

If you ever happen to be in Burla, you will see this 4.8-kilometre-long dam that connects Burla on one side with the Hirakud town on the other. On either side of the dam, in both towns, there are two tall constructions, which serve as lighthouses. The one in Burla is called Jawahar Minar, named after Pandit Jawaharlal Nehru, who, people say, came to visit the site while the dam was being built.

From the top of the Jawahar Minar, the view of the dam is breathtaking. The length of the dam holds back the huge water reserve of the river Mahanadi on the left, releasing it partially through the canals, from which the water passes through the gates on the right and flows further east, right through the Burla town. Giant pulleys along the length of the dam and a high-voltage electricity plant fill the scene in the east. In the south-west, there is a scattering of green islands rising out of the water. Looking in this direction, it appears as if there is no end to the water—it is hard to make out the line on the horizon, miles away, where the water meets the sky. The sound of the running turbine is the loudest noise one can hear. One can see the whirlpool of churning water as it drops down the open gates and goes ahead to rotate the turbine. On the east of this, stands my beautiful town Burla.

Back in my childhood days, everything about Burla was small. Anyone who owned a Maruti 800 was considered extremely rich. For what it was worth, only a handful of people were privileged enough to have this car in their garage. The town was so small that one could easily travel from one corner of it to another in less than half an hour, that too on a bicycle.

In spite of being tiny, Burla was pretty self-sufficient. We had just one market to shop from, which primarily was divided into two sub-markets. People used to call one the 'Kaccha Market' and other the 'Pakka Market'. There wasn't any difference in the infrastructures of these two markets, which could have been the reason why they were separated by names. The only difference was that the Kaccha Market was primarily a place to buy vegetables; while, just one hundred metres ahead, the Pakka Market was made up of a range of kiraana, grocery stores and clothes' stores. Come Sunday and the Kaccha Market would turn into the most populated area of the entire town. A number of small trucks and jeeps would bring in fresh vegetables in the morning, and everyone, including my father, would go to the Kaccha Market to buy them. But if someone had to buy anything big, like a home appliance or furniture, he had to travel to Sambalpur, the nearest city, because a wide variety of such things was usually not available in Burla.

The town was also treated as the knowledge hub of Orissa. In Burla there were Veer Surendra Sai (VSS) Medical College, one of the most well-known medical colleges in Orissa, and a well-to-do engineering college called University College of Engineering (UCE). Apart from the engineering and medical institutes, we also had a branch of Sambalpur University. As far as the primary and secondary education was concerned, there were three different schools, each of them affiliated to a different language medium—Hindi, Oriya and English. My parents had admitted me to the English-medium school. It was called Sri Sathya Sai Kiddies Abode.

Burla was a secular town and had religious institutions for

all the religions. Temples of Hindu gods, including Lord Ram, Lord Jagannath and Lord Krishna, provided the religious platform for the majority of the people. Every day a lot of devotees would visit these temples to pay homage to their deities. The biggest temple in the town was of Lord Krishna. It was well known as the Krishna Mandir, though it had idols of other gods and goddesses as well inside it. The yearly Janmashtami celebrations were held with great enthusiasm at the temple. Apart from the Hindu temples, there was a mosque at the Kaccha Market, a church near the road to Hirakud dam and a gurdwara right at the geographical heart of the town. And this was where I lived with my family.

My father worked in the gurdwara as a priest and our house was located within the gurdwara's complex. We were a family of four—my mother, my father, my younger brother and I. The entire complex was a vast rectangle, with the central portion of it taken up by the gurdwara building, surrounded by an open courtyard on three sides. Beyond the courtyard on both sides, a series of seven living quarters marked the boundary of the area. These quarters were owned by the gurdwara management, and the rent from them was one of the sources of revenue for the gurdwara.

To the front of the complex was the gateway to enter, and on the right corner was our house. Of course, it wasn't a house we owned, but a service house offered to my father because of his job at the gurdwara. It wasn't a well-planned house, but a good enough arrangement of brick and mortar, divided into four rooms. If you saw it, you would know what I mean when I say that it was barely meant to provide shelter. At the entrance itself was the kitchen; but because of the three chairs placed against one of the walls, it also served as a sitting room when the women from our neighbourhood occasionally turned up for a leisurely chat with my mother. The arrangement worked well for Mom, as she could cook while chatting with her friends.

Our second room was where we used to spend most of our time, and so, technically, we called it the living room. This room, every night after 9, turned into our bedroom. I guess I was in Class III when Dad bought a black-and-white Rohini Deluxe television set encased in a brown wooden box. It had shutters as well, which we would pull down at night and pull up again in the morning. It had slots for storing twelve channels, though there was only Doordarshan that all the antennas in Burla could tune to—so the rest of the channel slots were just a wastage of TV memory. Ever since the TV was brought into that room, we had started spending most of our time in there. I remember Dad watching the Hindi broadcast of Doordarshan news at 9 p.m., after which my brother and I used to watch serials along with Mom.

On one side of this room was a wooden cot which had an in-between kind of size. Its width was more than that of a single bed, but less than that of a double bed. A wooden dressing table and a multipurpose wooden table occupied the rest of the room. The table was primarily a study table, but we also used it as a dining table for all our meals. Mom even used to iron our clothes on it late in the afternoon.

When I look back, I see how we needed only a few things to keep ourselves happy. Apart from the bed and the table, our living room had a lot of free space. A three-feet-tall and five-feet-wide trunk served as the storage for all our requirements, for the winter and otherwise—blankets, mattresses, bed sheets, cushions and a lot of winter clothes like sweaters and things that we needed to use after long intervals. On the other side of the room, there was a closet with a glass door, full of religious books that my father used to read. My brother and I used the remaining space in that room to dance, fight and do all sorts of crazy things.

The last room was not quite a room, but actually functioned as a store. It was full of wooden logs to support the intermittent construction of the gurdwara building. Against one wall, there was a wooden rack holding large containers of rice, pickles and flour that Dad would have managed to get dirt cheap as part of a bulk purchase. A rope ran from one corner of the room to another. This was used to hang out clothes after Mom would have ironed them, for we didn't have an almirah to keep our clothes in.

Our house was tiny, simple and yet complex in its

arrangement. We loved to live there primarily because of the vast courtyard outside, where my brother and I used to play. No one in the entire Burla enjoyed as big a playground as we used to.

3

My World in Black and White

My brother and I had rhyming names. It was quite common in many families to do so. While my parents named me Ravinder, they named my brother Jitender. But the usage of these names was only limited to our school. At home, and, for that matter, in the rest of the town, we were known by our shorter names. I was called Rinku and my brother was called Tinku—rhyming pet names as well!

Tinku was two years younger to me, and, by the time he was getting admitted to nursery, I was getting into Class I in the same school. One of our oldest pictures—in which we are together for the very first time—goes back to this time. It shows us perched on a two-seater red tricycle at a photo studio. A day I can still clearly recall . . .

It was a Sunday and Mom had got us ready by the noon. She made us wear the new clothes she had bought only a day before. The two of us looked nice. We had first looked appreciatively at each other and then stared at our own selves in the mirror. As soon as we were about to leave, Mom applied some talcum powder on our faces with her handkerchief. I guess that was the make-up sure to make us look fairer!

After that, we proudly climbed on to Dad's bicycle. In no time, we were at a photography store in the Kaccha Market. We had been all excited knowing the fact that someone was going to take our pictures with a camera! It made us feel special, and, on top of it, our new clothes made us feel extra-special.

At the photographer's studio, Dad shook hands with the studio owner and exchanged a few words. All this while, Tinku and I were helping each other to tuck our T-shirts in and rearranging the creases of our half-pants.

When Dad called, we both ran inside the studio with him. We looked around wide-eyed. For us little boys, it was an amazingly beautiful place, full of the possibilities of all sorts of adventure. Till then, we'd only seen a studio from outside, and this one offered so many things to explore!

There were big stands with white umbrellas on them inclined at different angles. While the corners of the rooms were dark, the centre was fully illuminated with the light reflecting off those umbrellas. There was a lot of light in that space, much more than we would have seen at our home.

My brother and I ran around in the studio and explored everything. There were wires running here and there on the ground. The wall in front of us had a number of background options. They were a sort of curtains. We pulled out a few to see how they looked, and then pulled out a few more. There was a dressing table with a mirror in one corner, along with a small plastic comb that had a few missing teeth, some talcum powder and a few lipsticks. All those items smelled bad, so I kept them back as soon as I lifted them. There was a huge carton in another corner of the room. It was way above our height, so we could not find out what was in there. At that time we didn't know that the box contained something that would change our lives forever!

Soon, the door opened and someone walked in. He said hello to us. There was a camera hanging from his neck. He was our cameraman. He was paying us so much attention because we were special for him. And, sure enough, he told us that he had got something for us. While we wondered what he was talking about, he walked towards the big carton at the other end of the room and pulled out a red kids' tricycle for us.

'Oh, wow!' Tinku shouted. Then, as soon as the cameraman placed the tricycle at the centre of the room, he ran to grab his seat on it.

I too ran after Tinku. We were about to enter into a

scuffle when the cameraman intervened and shifted Tinku to the back seat. I loved the cameraman when he did so! Tinku protested, but the cameraman told him that the one who would sit on the back seat would look better in the photo. I silently thanked the cameraman for being secretly on my side. So my brother took the rear seat without protest, while I sat in front and jammed my feet into the pedals. Somehow, the front seat with the handle in my hands made me feel more powerful and special!

Sitting on that tricycle, with the umbrella lights focused on us, we were the centre of attention for the cameraman and our father. We took a considerable amount of time to settle down well. It wasn't easy to stay put in one spot, or to hold a pose. But the cameraman was an expert. He kept on guiding us and then suddenly he said, 'Smile karo baccha log,' and we did, and he clicked us.

But our smiles did not last long. They vanished as soon as we realized that this place wasn't a toy shop selling that cute red tricycle to us. It was only a photo studio, and that tricycle was a prop belonging to the studio owner. We never wanted to get up from that tricycle. We wanted to pedal it down to our home.

'Daddy, asi eh chalaa ke ghar javaange na?' [Daddy, we are going to ride this to home, right?] Tinku asked, trying to establish our claim over it.

Dad laughed along with the cameraman and explained to us, while pulling us out, that it wasn't our tricycle to take home. As soon as Tinku heard this, he gripped the front seat and almost dug his feet into the ground, retaliating at Dad's attempt to pull him out. While I'd understood the truth and got off, my brother was screaming and shouting. Dad tried to scare him with his big eyes and also raised his forefinger to his lips and said, 'Shhhhh . . .' It was a warning for him to stop shouting and behave himself.

And thankfully, in no time, his melodrama was over.

I held Tinku's hand in mine as the two of us followed Dad out of the room. The red tricycle remained in the centre of the room, alone, surrounded by the focused umbrella lights. It was heartbreaking to leave that beautiful toy there.

But I will never forget my younger brother's eyes in those last moments, when Dad was making the payment at the counter on the other side of the room. As the two of us stood next to Dad, another family with two kids entered the studio. The same cameraman led them to the same tricycle. The kids joyfully ran towards it and climbed up the seats of the tricycle, which was only a few moments back Rinku and Tinku's tricycle—*our* tricycle. The parents lovingly adjusted the positions of their kids on the tricycle. It was as if, right in front of our eyes, those kids were celebrating their victory.

My brother stood calmly and watched everything without blinking. I watched that family, and then turned to look at my brother. I felt protective of him. It hurt me that he had wanted something so much, and yet he couldn't have it.

Soon Dad was through with the payment and asked us to follow him back home. I remember saying those final words to my brother as I continued to hold his hand, 'Ae taa chhoti tricycle hai. Asi taa vaddi cycle lavaange!' [This is a small tricycle. We will buy a bigger one!] It was my way of consoling him. With that, I tightened my grip over his hand and we walked out of the studio.

'Heads, I will stay back. Tails, you will,' he suggests.

The sound of gunfire and the boulders behind which they are hiding, in the hills, fill in the entire scene.

He tosses the coin.

It's heads.

Jai shows the coin on his palm to Veeru, and asks him to immediately leave along with Basanti, and come back with four cartons of ammunition.

Soon, he is all by himself, fighting the bandits on the plateau. I believe he will make it. I believe he will kill everyone—the way he has done so far.

But the next time he opens the chamber of his revolver, there is only one bullet in it. Something tells me that he is going to do wonders with that one bullet. He has to.

That is when he spots a bomb over the wooden bridge, which is the only connection between him and the bandits. But time is running out. The bandits have already stepped on to that bridge, and are making their way towards him.

He has all my attention. It is a dangerous moment. I love Jai and I want him to win. But he is all alone. I cross my fingers. I shout and tell him to wait and not to come out into the open. He is safe there behind the rocks.

Besides, I am furious at Veeru, who hasn't yet come back with the ammunition. *'Veeru kyun nahi aa raha?'* I shout and leap up, wondering why Veeru hasn't showed up.

Just then, from behind the rock, Jai jumps out into the open to pick up an abandoned revolver.

'Oh no, Jai!' I shout and inch closer to the TV set.

His body rolls in the dust. A few more rounds of fire are heard. I am worried about Jai. I pray to God for his safety. He picks up that revolver and walks straight to the bridge. The bandits are advancing from the other side.

'Oh God!' I say and grab my forehead in my hands.

Jai takes an aim at the bomb with his revolver in the left hand. Right then, I see a spot of blood oozing out of his body.

'Shit! Goli lag gayi Jai ko!' I scream—Jai has been shot.

An injured Jai shoots at the bomb. It explodes, and the bridge collapses. A few bandits are killed, while the rest of them run away.

The blood-soaked Jai is lying on the ground. Veeru arrives on his horse and calls out Jai's name.

My heart sinks to see Jai lying like that in Veeru's lap. He says that he won't be able to tell their stories to Veeru's children. That confirms he is not going to survive. I am about to break down. I still pray to God that my fear should not come true.

Jai continues to mutter Veeru's name before he finally takes his last breath.

He dies. My hero dies. My Jai dies.

The sad tune of the harmonica that Jai used to play follows his death. And I start crying. Tears roll down my eyes. I grieve for the loss of Jai. I finish watching the rest of the movie in a state of deep agony. If the Thakur wouldn't have finished Gabbar off, I had pledged to find that beast and avenge Jai's death by killing him myself.

I spend a sad day thinking about Jai. Occasionally, I cry. Later in the evening, when my father is watching the news in the prime-time bulletin, I spot Jai in one of the news items.

I can't believe my eyes. I shout, 'Jai is alive?'

Dad looks at me and asks, 'Why? What happened to him? And his name is Amitabh Bachchan!'

'No, he is Jai! He died this afternoon,' I say, my eyes still focused on the man on the screen. There are a lot of people around him. He is signing something for them and smiling.

'He watched Sholay today and the character's death in the movie has made him sad,' Mom updates Dad.

He bursts into laughter.

Dad then explains to me that movies and serials are just fiction. News is for real. I listen to him very carefully.

Just before going to bed, I go to Dad. He is in his bed and fast asleep. But this can't wait. I wake him up from his sleep and ask, 'Daddy, you're sure Jai is alive, na?'

4

Fear of the Needle

If there was anything that I was afraid of as a child, it was the hospital in our town. The hospital building was the biggest structure of brick and concrete in Burla—a light pink colour, and surrounded by tall green deodars and gulmohar trees, with seasonal orange flowers in them. A never-ending row of bicycles and motorcycles would make a serpentine line in the shade of the trees.

Every time I crossed that building, I used to feel a chill run down my spine. From the outside, everything was just so quiet and normal. But only the people who would have walked into it would know about what happened inside. I had walked into it a couple of times.

I was made to do so, against my will, by my father.

So I knew what went on inside.

My brother and I had not been given our inoculations at birth or in the few months afterwards, as was the usual practice. Our tragedy was that by the time our parents realized the importance of those injections, we were old enough to understand that injections hurt. Therefore, we used to run away from them.

But they were necessary.

So Dad, very cunningly, never told us when he was taking us to the hospital. He would make the two of us sit on his bicycle and tell us that we were going out for a nice ride. Tinku, as usual, would occupy the front bar while I would sit on the carrier, holding on to the front seat, on which Dad would be sitting. Only when he would miss the right turn towards the Pakka Market and continue to go straight, where the road led to nothing but the hospital, we would be clear of his ill intentions.

And then suddenly my brother and I would start squirming on our seats, knowing what was coming our way.

'Daddy, assi kitthey jaa rahe hain?' [Daddy, where are we going?] one of us would ask in a terrified tone, very much aware of the answer.

It was quite common for our father to not provide an answer to that one. So I would tell my brother, 'Tinku, Daddy saanu injection lagvaan lae ke jaa rahe hai.' [Tinku, Daddy is taking us for our injections.]

And then my brother would ask, 'But Daddy had told us that we were going for a ride?'

So I would tell him, 'Daddy ne jhutt boleya si.' [Daddy had lied to us.]

'Rinku Veer, Daddy ne jhutt kyun boleya si?' [Why did Daddy lie?] he would ask again, trying to reconfirm the unbelievable.

The bicycle would keep moving. The two of us would keep talking. I always wanted to hold my brother's hand then. He too would want to see me. But the two of us used to be separated by our father.

Right at the registration counter, our fear would take a mammoth shape. The clerk at the registration desk knew our father very well. He would smile and fill in half the details on his own. Our father would take two slips, one for each of us, and we would walk with him, holding his hands on either side—the two of us in our half-pants and T-shirts, ready to be poked!

As we walked up the staircase, I would realize how close we were to the terrible process. The peculiar smell of disinfectant would fill my nostrils and virtually choke me. The dark galleries of the hospital's outdoor wards would terrorize me. The sight of the green curtains, the nurses in white and the number of sick people around would make me also feel sick. The whole atmosphere in that government hospital was that of a horror story.

That horror multiplied by several times the moment we would reach our ward. As usual, there would be a vampire-like nurse whose business it was to draw blood from people's fingers or arms, besides injecting poor little kids like us. We knew her well. She was acquainted with us too. We were a challenge for her. Many times, we had created a scene in front of her and the rest of the hospital, crying, screaming and running out without our pants!

Knowing our desperation to escape, Dad never forgot to lure us with items of our interest. Most of the times, he would tempt us by saying that he was going to treat us to Frooti—a popular mango drink—if only we agreed to take the shots.

We were madly in love with that three-rupee drink, which came packaged in a square green Tetra Pak. The front of the packet had an image of two ripe, yellow mangoes, with droplets of chilled water sliding down them. Dad knew very well how much we loved this particular drink. Insane as it might sound, our deep love for Frooti overcame our fear of the injections, and our father knew how to use that.

We would willingly lie down on our stomachs on the medical bed, baring our bottoms for the injections. In our minds, we would see the shopkeeper taking the chilled packets of Frooti out of his freezer, just for us. In the meantime, the nurse would take out the needle from the boiling water over the electric heater. Our dreams would progress, and we would now be holding our coveted drink in our hands. The nurse was constantly in the process of preparing the injection, pushing in the nozzle to flush the air out of the syringe. And, as we imagined piercing the tiny round foil at the upper corner of the Tetra Pak with our pointed straws, the nurse would pierce our behinds with that injection.

The reality of that moment, for the next few seconds, would break our reverie and leave us in great pain. But, we knew, the key for us was to keep holding on to our thoughts, to relish them enough to be able to overlook reality. Soon it would all be over, yet we continued to lie there, exactly in the same posture, happily imagining sipping our Frootis, smiling! Two brothers, lying half-naked on their stomach, with their eyes glued to a daydream and smiles pasted on their faces!

And that's when the nurse would shout, 'Utth jaao. Ho gaya!' [Get up. It's done!]

In the next half an hour, we would make our dreams come true—with a bang. Our experience of drinking Frooti would not just end there at the shop. It was a ritual for us to bring that empty Tetra Pak back home with us. We would blow as much air as possible into it with the straw, place the inflated packet on the ground and ask everyone around us to watch as we jumped over our packets. *Bang!*—It would burst like a cracker. That would mark the completion of our Frooti adventure!

If, by any chance, the packet didn't burst at the first go, we would not shy away from picking it up and going on and on, until it finally gave way.

5

All for a Toothy Grin!

One day, Dad took me for a visit to the hospital again. He told me that my injection course had been completed, and so I could relax. *But how could I relax—when I was being taken into that same building?* I was only convinced when he took a different staircase this time, leading to a different wing. I had never been to this part of the hospital earlier. Yet, I was sceptical. After all, injections weren't the only thing I hated, it was the entire hospital.

Dad took me straight to the dental outdoor ward. There was already a long queue there. Dad handed over the ticket to the compounder, who placed it underneath the stack of tickets on the doctor's table. He then placed a paperweight over the pile, and went back to relax on the stool by the door.

I wondered why we were there. I looked at the people around me. They all had their mouths closed, so I could not get to know what sort of dental problems they had. Which made me wonder—*What sort of a problem did I have?* Everything was fine with me. I had neither complained of any toothache, nor did I have foul breath.

So I asked my father, 'Daddy, you have a problem with your teeth?'

'Ki?' [What?] he asked, absent-mindedly.

'Tuhadde dand kharaab hain?' [Something is wrong with your teeth?] I asked him in Punjabi this time.

He laughed and shook his head, 'Nahi, nahi!'

'Taa fer assi aithe kyun aaye, haan?' I asked, wondering why we were there, in that case.

My father sat me down and told me the reason why we were in the dental ward. My front two milk teeth had fallen a few months back. The gap should ideally have been filled up by a pair of brand new, permanent teeth. My family kept expecting this act of nature to happen by itself. But nature had been probably too busy with other things, and forgotten me. So we needed a doctor, who could become nature's proxy for me.

About half an hour later the doctor called my name: 'Ravinder Singh!'

My father flung into action. He asked me to quickly put back on the rubber slippers that had fallen off my hanging feet. Together, we rushed inside the room. The room was bright with sunrays, which flooded into it from a spacious window behind the dentist. There was a person sitting next to the dentist, with a black bag on his lap. Once in a while, he pulled out a medicine from it and kept talking about it to the dentist.

Dad told me that this man was a medical representative. I don't know what exactly he wanted, but the dentist did not seem even a bit interested in his talk. The only time the dentist looked at him was when he placed a nice-looking pen set, a diary and a calendar on his table.

Looking at them, the dentist asked, 'The same things again?'

The medical representative slipped his hand inside his bag again and brought out a plastic torch, which he placed on the table with a huge smile. Soon after this, he left. I wondered why he'd spent so much time explaining about the medicines when the real thing the dentist was interested in was that torch!

I looked around. The walls around me had neatly labelled diagrams of jaws and teeth. The words 'incisor', 'canine', 'molar' and 'pre-molar' in one of the pictures appeared familiar to me. I had read about them in my science class. I wanted to show my father my brilliance. So I tugged at his hand, wanting to tell him that we should tell the dentist that my incisors had failed to develop. But he ignored me and continued to explain the problem himself.

I continued to look at the decorated walls. There was a

poster of a beautiful lady with glittering white teeth. She had a tube of white-and-red striped toothpaste in her hand. She had a beautiful smile. Now, finally, the dentist looked at me, and asked me to open my mouth. I smiled, imitating the smile of the lady in the poster. The dentist, unimpressed, asked me to look towards him and not towards the poster.

'Don't smile, Ravinder, open your mouth. Like this— aaaaaaaa!' he showed me how to do it. He looked funny.

I'd guessed the smile was a nice way to reveal my teeth, including the absent ones. However, this time I opened my mouth as wide as possible and sang, 'Aaaaaaaaa!' as loud as possible. I made my tongue dance to the sound.

As I held my mouth wide open for the longest time, my eyes seemed to shrink and my cheeks were stretched. I had invested a lot of energy in sustaining that show. Everyone around me was looking at me.

'Okay, okay, this is enough,' the dentist finally said.

I closed my mouth and turned my attention back to the smiling lady with the toothpaste. The dentist explained a few things to my father, which I completely ignored. He prescribed some medicine for me and asked us to visit him again after two days. The last thing I heard him saying was that the procedure would take an hour when we visited next, so I would have to miss a period or two at school.

I checked with Dad if he was going to do anything to me, and whether it was going to be painful. Dad shook his head—all I had to do was to take the medicines and come and show the doctor my teeth, the way I'd done today. I realized that after two days I could legitimately bunk school!

For the next two days, each meal I ate was followed by a medicine.

On Day Three, I looked at myself in the mirror while brushing my teeth to see if, by any chance, the medicines had worked and I had new teeth.

Nothing! The inside of my mouth appeared, more or less, just as it had two days back. *Paagal dentist*, I told myself in the mirror.

At school, I proudly told all my friends that I would be there for only half the day. I was going to bunk the second half! Dad was there right on time to pick me up, and, as my classmates watched with envy, I quickly put my schoolbag on my shoulders and ran to Dad.

It all started exactly the way it had started the other day. We first got a slip made, took the other staircase and walked through the other wing and arrived at the outdoor dental ward, where a lot of people were waiting in the queue. I peeped inside the dentist's room to see if the lady with that glittering smile was still there on the wall. Yep, she was right there!—still smiling and still holding that toothpaste.

'Shall we start, then?' the doctor looked at my father and asked, after they had discussed a few things.

Dad nodded, without looking at me.

The dentist called for a nurse and asked me to follow her. I looked at Dad's face. His silence rang a warning bell in my head. Though I followed the nurse, there were a lot of thoughts in my mind. She led me to a vacant cabin on the extreme right of the dental ward.

In no time, I found myself sitting on a long reclining chair. The nurse referred to it as the dentist's chair, and adjusted it for me. She pulled a lever, it leant back. She pulled another one, and I was above the ground. I asked her what was on her mind. She didn't say a single extra word.

Meanwhile, the dentist appeared. As he came closer to me, I watched him slip his hands into a pair of gloves. He then strapped on a mask. Watching that made me sure that something terrible was in store for me. I was trapped in that elevated reclining chair. I asked the dentist what was going to happen.

'We are going to bring your teeth out of your gums,' he replied.

'What?!' I asked. And, when no one answered, I asked again, 'How?'

'We will have to make a small cut in your gums.'

And he dropped a bomb into my open mouth.

'You are going to cut my gums? No! Please! It's going to hurt!' I yelled.

The dentist and the nurse ignored me.

I asked them to call my father. They still ignored me.

The dentist and the nurse were now almost ready to dissect my tiny, pink gums. The nurse adjusted the overhead light so that it fell right on my face. It blurred my vision for a second. The dentist picked up his tools and asked me to open my mouth.

I was petrified.

'No, no! It's going to hurt!' I kept repeating. My legs trembled. I wanted to get off that reclining chair and escape, but it was impossible to get off.

The dentist said it wouldn't hurt, because he was going to give me anaesthesia. As he mentioned that, he picked up a large injection. It had a long needle that would have been around four inches, if not five. He brandished that horrible thing right in front of my scared eyes.

I froze. I couldn't utter a single thing. I was staring at the injection.

'Daddyyyyyyyy!' I cried out. No, I screamed!

It was probably the loudest and the longest scream of my entire life. I'm quite sure it could be heard much beyond that small cabin, the dental ward, travelling down the staircase right into the parking lot. In its long journey, my scream must have announced my panic to almost everyone present in that hospital, including my father.

In no time, Dad came running into the cabin. He looked at the dentist and the nurse. They had left whatever they had been holding so far. Their hands were on their ears. It was all only too clear.

The dentist looked at my father and didn't feel the need to say anything. My father apologized on my behalf. I looked at my father and begged him to take me away. He patted my back and told me that it was important that I allow the dentist to operate on my mouth. He explained that if this was not done, I would be left toothless for the rest of my life.

'I am fine with that! I don't want this! Please, Daddy!' I had begun to cry.

'You won't even get to know. It won't hurt at all after you take this anaesthesia,' the dentist pitched in.

It took me a minute to frame my answer. 'Oh God! How dumb! This anaesthesia injection itself is going to hurt, na!'

The nurse smiled. The dentist looked angrily at her.

The dentist turned to Dad and announced, 'If you can't convince him now, you will have to bring him next week, as I have other cases to look after.'

I thought of telling him to postpone it. But, right then, Dad recalled that next week he would be out of station. So the operation had to be done that day itself.

Half an hour later, with me on that dentist's chair, our negotiations and peace talks had failed. The outcome of this failure was simple. We were at war!

United, they stood. Alone, I sat.

Dad asked the dentist to proceed with my operation. The dentist again picked up his syringe and filled it. I took up my attacking position. The moment the dentist came close to me, I punched into the air between us, narrowly missing the injection. Dad shouted at me and asked the nurse to pin down one of my arms. He then grabbed my other arm.

The goddamn chair didn't even allow me to jump off!

I wildly paddled my legs in the air. A few cotton balls, along with a few dental instruments, fell over the big arm of the chair. And I screamed my lungs out. It was not only difficult, but almost impossible, for the dentist to inject me. He kept shouting that if I didn't stop, my struggling might end up in the needle breaking and getting stuck somewhere inside my gum. But that didn't bother me. I screamed out louder in response. We were caught in a tussle. It was three versus one—the little me, to be precise.

The three of them were shouting too, telling each other what to do.

Dad then asked the nurse to pin down both my hands. He twisted my arms and brought my hands together, behind the back of the chair, and asked the nurse to hold them down in that position. He then went to the other side of the reclining chair, to hold down my legs. He sat on my knees and weighed down my thighs. My legs were now in his full control.

I gathered up all my energy and continued to protest. The tight grip of the nurse had almost stopped the blood circulation in my wrists. I was now sweating. I felt suffocated—but I didn't give up. My eyes had grown big and red. But my idea was not to settle down, and keep continuing my fight. But in no time, I was exhausted. I was breathing heavily. The three of them knew this. They could see that, every moment, I was getting a little more tired. When my revolt was reduced to intermittent screams, the dentist came closer to me.

My father and the nurse continued to hold me tight. The dentist told them that he was finally going to inject me. I collected all my leftover energy and, now, instead of moving my body, I started shaking my head left and right.

The dentist was now extremely irritated. So was my father. The nurse kept shouting, just out of my line of sight, 'Kya kar rahe ho, beta! Aise mat karo.' [What are you doing, son! Don't act like this.]

The dentist went out for a moment and brought his compounder with him. Mercilessly, he commanded the compounder to hold my head and restrain any sort of movement. He also instructed him to hold my face in such a way that my jaws would remain wide apart. So this was now four versus one.

The compounder attempted to do what he was told. But the moment his hands crawled on to my jaw, I bit him hard. His hands tasted of Dettol, the disinfectant. I immediately spat out, and the spit landed on the dentist's apron. The compounder yelled in pain. The dentist shrieked out of frustration. Dad continued to shout at me. The nurse kept saying, 'Beta, beta . . .'

After a half-an-hour-long battle, my body gave up. I wanted air to breathe, a lot of it. I had fought like a braveheart. But I was now exhausted and had resigned myself to fate. I closed my eyes when I saw the syringe inches away from me. I felt the tears from my eyes and the sweat on my face mingling together.

The next thing I felt was an intense pain that surged up from my gums to somewhere behind my nose. I could feel the dentist emptying his syringe somewhere inside the tissues and nerves behind my nostrils. There was pin-drop silence in the cabin. After taking the injection out of my mouth, the doctor wrapped a plastic body cover around me.

I remained calm. Two streams of tears rolled down my cheeks.

The anaesthesia was quick in its work. I could soon feel a heaviness in my gums. I opened my eyes and looked at Dad. He told me it was all fine. I looked at his hands. They were still pinning down my thighs. I looked back into his eyes. I didn't say anything. I didn't want to say anything.

I closed my wet eyes and remained calm for the rest of the procedure.

After about twenty minutes, the dentist tapped my shoulder and told me, 'It's all over. You can get up.'

I opened my eyes, but, this time, I didn't make any eye contact with him. I had heard what he had said, yet I didn't move. I ignored it and him.

The nurse let go of my hands. My father got up and came closer to me. He assured me that the operation was over. He patted my shoulder, in an attempt to comfort me. I didn't make any eye contact with him either. Nor did I speak.

When he asked me to get up, I didn't move. When he left me alone and went away to consult the dentist about what I should eat and what I shouldn't, I got up unnoticed and walked out of the room.

While walking out of the cabin, I came across a washbasin with a mirror installed on the wall above it. I looked at myself. My nose and lips were still inflated. There were a few bloodstains on my shirt and around my lips. I tried to open my mouth. I wasn't able to feel anything. The effect of the anaesthesia was still there. I was merely able to pull down my lower lip. I saw cotton stuffed in my mouth, surrounding my front upper gums.

The dentist shouted from behind me: 'No! Don't take the cotton out!'

I tucked my T-shirt into my shorts and walked out of the room alone. In the meantime, Dad had finished his conversation with the dentist and followed me out.

'Chalo, ghar chalein,' [Let's go home] he said, and took my hand.

I didn't say anything but followed him—

—but not before slipping my fingers out of his hands.

6

The Question of Birth

It was late in the night on my seventh birthday when the most intriguing thought of my life crossed my mind. Mom had switched off the lights long back and I was in my bed. Day-long celebrations of my birthday and the euphoria of it all had left me quite tired by the end of the day.

Yet, I was awake. My eyes were focused on the fluorescent minute and hour hands of the clock on the dark wall in front of me. Technically, in the next fifteen minutes my birthday would be over. So I was revisiting the series of events of that special day.

It had been a perfect birthday. In the morning, Dad had said special prayers on my behalf in the gurdwara. At school, I was the only student who wasn't in his uniform but in his new birthday clothes. I was the one for whom the entire class sang *Happy birthday to you*, and, in return, I had distributed chocolates to my classmates and my teachers.

In the evening, for the very first time, I had cut a cake on my birthday. Till then, cake-cutting wasn't a practice that my family followed. After many requests from me, my parents had agreed to a cake-cutting ceremony. So Mom had borrowed an oven from someone in the neighbourhood and baked the cake for me. It had seven cherries on the top. For my cake-cutting ceremony, I had made sure that I invited only those friends of mine who would bring gifts for me. For dinner, Mom had made my favourite rajma chaawal. It was a beautiful day and I wished for it to never end. And yet here it was, slipping out of my fingers . . .

As soon as both the hands of the clock hit twelve, I closed my eyes with the pleasant feeling that it had been seven years since my birth.

. . . seven years!

. . . since I was born!

. . . SEVEN years . . . like . . . one . . . two . . . three . . . four . . . five . . . six . . . SEVEN years!

. . . since I was born!

But how the hell was I born? And my eyes flashed open.

It occurred to me suddenly. *Yes! But how the hell had I been born?* I thought to myself.

Seven years had passed and this thought had never struck my mind, ever! All of a sudden, in the darkness of that night, the fact that I didn't know how I had arrived on this planet started bothering me. Never before had my own existence in this world been as thrilling for me as it became on that very night.

I spent the next few minutes tackling my anxiety. I pacified myself by thinking that there was nothing to worry about, and that I would soon find out how I was born. However, sleep had run miles away from me. The Einstein in me had raised his head, and I needed this complex mystery of How I Had Evolved to be unveiled.

I had some vague thoughts and theories of my own.

Maybe Mom had planted a seed in our garden and I came out of the plant!

Maybe I had been dropped from the sky during the rainy season. If not that, then maybe . . .

These thoughts were all products of my wondering mind in the middle of the night, but none of them appeared convincing enough to me. I kept tossing and turning in bed, turning over the thoughts again and again.

Almost an hour later, too restless to stay in bed, I sat up. I looked at my mother, who was sleeping along with Tinku on the bed next to mine. I then looked at Tinku and wondered—*How had I missed noticing when Tinku was born?* He arrived two years after me! I spent the next few minutes regretting how I had missed my glorious chance to solve this puzzle. I juggled between wanting to wake Mom up to ask her my question, and resisting myself and going back to sleep.

I finally chose not to wake her up, so I went back to my bed.

But the excitement didn't let me sleep. Five minutes later, I got up from the bed again. I looked at Mom, again. Barefoot and in my pajamas and vest, I walked towards Mom. When I reached her side of the bed, I stood close to her face.

She was in deep sleep. I was in deep anxiety.

'Mommy!' I whispered.

Nothing happened.

'MOMMY!' I whispered louder.

'Hmm . . .' Mom murmured in her sleep.

I was too scared to wake her up.

'M-o-m-m-y.' I didn't whisper, but called her aloud this time.

And she woke up with a start. 'H-a-a-n!'

She was scared. She looked at me and then at the clock, and realized that she had been asleep and I had just woken her up.

Worried, she got up and asked, 'Ki hogaya, beta?' [What happened, baby?]

All of a sudden, I struggled to frame my question. I rubbed my right foot against my left leg.

'Ki hogaya, haan?' she asked again, trying to ensure that I was all right.

This time, I rubbed my nose and eyes with my fingers. For a while, I even forgot why I had woken her up.

She asked if I wanted to go to the bathroom. I shook my head from left to right to indicate the negative.

'Phir?' She seemed to be getting impatient. My brother, in his sleep, shifted from the right to the left.

'Mommy!' I managed to utter.

'Haan, bol?' [Yes, ask?]

'Mommy, mein kis tarah peda hoya si?' I blurted out my question—How was I born?

I stared intently at her face but could not read her facial expressions.

There was a smile on her lips.

There was confusion in between the lines of her forehead.

7

Life's Greatest Mystery Solved!

It took me three more weeks to crack the biggest mystery of my life till then. Unfortunately, and I don't know why, no one was ready to share the truth with me. I had trusted my mother when she had said that she didn't know how I was born, because she'd found me in the gurdwara one day.

But I stopped believing her when, on verifying, I got a different answer from my father. He said that he too didn't know how I had arrived on this planet, as he had bought me from a shop which was far away from home.

Liars! Both of them!

All those evasive answers had only intensified my curiosity to know the truth about my birth. On the one hand, it all appeared like a secret conspiracy to me; even though, on the other, I didn't quite reject the possibility that a natural calamity had, by some means, thrown me into this world. I kept thinking of this all the time—on my way to school, between classes, in my bed before falling asleep, and the very next morning with a fresh mind while squatting over the toilet.

By the end of the second week, my curiosity had spiralled into an enormous question. It occupied my mind so badly that I was not able to focus on my school lessons. It was strange how it played on my mind continuously. Every time I thought about giving my brain a break by not thinking about it any more, I found myself doing the exact opposite in the next half an hour. It was as if I was addicted to it. At one time, I thought my brain would explode, struggling over the permutation and combination that it had been doing since the past two weeks. I reached a stage where I had to get it out of my system. So, finally, I decided to share my question with some of my classmates. Who knew, perhaps they were going through a similar dilemma, or perhaps they had an answer? One day, at recess, as we munched on the food from our tiffin boxes, I brought up the subject with a few friends who I was close to. While none of the boys had an answer to my question, a girl called Pinky had a startling insight to offer.

'You have come from your mommy's stomach,' she answered casually, and continued to eat her lunch. I stared at her, shocked. She knew this big secret, and was acting as if knowing it wasn't a big deal at all!

Also, it troubled me that a girl knew all about a subject which I knew nothing about; or, for that matter, none of the boys did! How could a girl know about it and not a boy? The male chauvinist in me felt insulted. The other boys seemed to have no such ego problems about Pinky's claim. They were busy eating from their tiffins. They didn't seem to be affected by it all!

I waited and tried to digest it all. I gulped down my prejudice and turned my thoughts to what Pinky had actually said. For some reason, I believed her theory. Perhaps it had been the confidence with which she had said it. I was feeling a little relieved. Till suddenly our friend Mandeep inquisitively quipped between bites, 'But how did he arrive in his mommy's stomach?'

Now that was a smart question! Chewing with concentration, I watched Pinky intently. *What was she going to say now?*

But she didn't say anything immediately. She paused for a bit, rolled her eyes and then turned to me and asked, 'Oh, yes! How *did* you get inside your mother's stomach?'

The others caught on to the ignorance she was trying to hide. 'Hey! Isko bhi nahi pata . . .' Mandeep made fun of her, pointing out that even she did not know.

'Ae, phek rahi thi . . . phek rahi thi . . .' [Hey, she was fibbing! She was fibbing!] the other boys mocked Pinky, and got back to eating their lunch, satisfied in the knowledge that she didn't actually know more than any of them.

The bell rang and we all got up to wash our hands. Pinky hadn't managed to finish her meal. While I rushed to the washroom, she merely walked, probably thinking over the debate that had just been raised.

I saw her on my way back from the washroom and realized that my feelings for her had changed all of a sudden. I empathized with her. At least she offered me something which I believed in or *could* believe in. She was better than my parents, who always started their answers with: 'I don't know, because we got you from here and there!' *Crap*.

At last, the school ended, and, then, the day ended. But my query still remained. It had now only spread from one person to two people—Pinky and I. But, as they say, where there is a will there is a way, and we too discovered our way by the end of the third week. But not before Pinky and I became really good friends! She had not brushed aside my question. She too was equally interested now in solving my mystery.

~

As I said, by the end of the third week since my birthday, I found myself very close to having this mystery solved. It was a Sunday—needless to say, one of the most enlightening Sundays of my life! This took place after *Rangoli*, a programme on Hindi film songs that used to air on Doordarshan. Mom had given both of us—my brother and me—a head bath.

Now, for us Sardar kids, Sundays used to hold a different meaning from everyone else. Besides all the fun of a holiday, Sundays for us came along with the cumbersome task of washing our long hair. It was a routine that Mom refused to let go of. She would carefully undo the buns on our heads, make us bend our heads and let the hair tumble down, before rigorously applying shampoo. The most difficult part was to hold my head in that bent position over a long time. The smell of Clinic Plus shampoo dominated the bathroom on this day of the week. But the ritual of the head bath didn't just end with the shampoo. After the bath, Mom would make us sit in the sun in order to dry out our hair. Most of the times, she would serve us breakfast in the sun. And, once she was free from the chores of the kitchen, she would apply coconut oil to our hair. Then it would be again put into a bun, and another week would pass before we went through the same process. My brother and I would joyfully watch *The Jungle Book* on TV as the oiling and tying up went on.

But that Sunday, there was no sun outside. Also, the servant who used to sweep the gurdwara compound every morning had arrived late. Mom was afraid that if he started cleaning the compound, the dust and dirt would get into our hair again. So she asked the two of us to come inside.

Even better.

We promptly plonked ourselves in front of the TV, our wet hair open and spread over the towels draped on the chair backs, with tiny water droplets rattling down the strands of our hair, forming a little pool of shampoo-scented water on the floor. To top it off, Mom had served us a piping hot breakfast of paranthas along with curd, with salt and pepper sprinkled nicely over it. We ate like happy brothers; our legs paddling in the air, our fingers and lips smacked with curd, and, at times, the two of us fighting to grab the next parantha that Mom would bring in from the kitchen.

This was indeed the good life—no school, no classes, only TV and playing!

Right at nine o'clock, like on every other Sunday, Mom brought in the last two paranthas for herself, along with some tea. While she readied herself to watch the most-watched television show of India, *Mahabharat*, my brother and I prepared ourselves to sing along with the title track. It was a part of our regular Sunday routine, which drove our mother nuts, but was a lot of fun.

With our eyes closed, we chorused in unison and rendered the track in our highest possible pitch: '. . . Sambhavaami yugeyyy yugeyyyyyyyyyyyyy!'

Our uncalled-for performance continued till that time-machine guy began with the same boring introduction: 'Main Samay hoon,' and that's when Mom shouted, 'Bus, haan! Chup ho jaao tussi doven.' [Enough, now! Stop, you two.]

Tinku and I looked at each other and giggled with our hands over our mouths. We whispered and made fun of the time-machine chap. We used to call him HMT, after the

name of the popular brand of wristwatches. I had no idea
what Mom liked so much about watching those planets
travelling here and there and listening to the silhouette of
the time-machine guy. There used to be a wheel with four
spokes as well, much like a wheel of a chariot. It would
zoom in and out.

Tinku and I watched *Mahabharat* mainly for the battle
scenes, especially because these were wars with charmed
bows and arrows. It was fascinating for us to watch how, at
times, the arrows would rain from the sky, and, at other
times, they would change into snakes. It was a mix of sci-fi
with the world of mythology. The forest scenes, too, held a
lot of interest for us. We loved it when the monsters with
magical powers were beaten up by the kings. The rest of
Mahabharat, for us, was a boring wait for *The Jungle Book*,
DuckTales and *TaleSpin*, which were the next shows in line.

That day, the episode of *Mahabharat* had neither any battle
scene, nor anything in the forests; but it turned out to be
one of the most revelatory in my life. This happened when I
learnt about the intention of the Sun God to bless Kunti, the
wife of King Pandu, with a baby.

'Chup ho ja, please!' I shouted to Tinku, when he insisted
I go out and play with him. *How could I?* I had just seen a ray
of hope! Here was my chance to find out how a baby was
produced, that too live on national television! *Who cared to
play?*

I can never forget that episode. Kunti had a spherical

water vessel of brass in her hand as she walked to the window of her beautifully decorated, luxurious room. She stretched her arms outside the window and gazed at that bright morning sun in the sky. She tilted the vessel and water flowed out of it to the ground. She closed her eyes and recited something—some kind of a mantra. I observed her lips but failed to decipher any part of it.

Right then, something happened that was difficult to digest for me, even at that age. A man, dressed in fine robes, walked out of the sun. He walked down to Kunti on an invisible staircase.

'Surya Devta . . .' Kunti whispered to herself.

'Sun God,' I whispered to my brother. My eyes were glued to our black-and-white TV set.

'Mowgli kab aayega?' Tinku inquired aloud about *The Jungle Book*.

'Thappad pe jaana hai tainnu, chup ho ja!' Mom repeated her favourite line—warning us to shut up, or else we would get slapped.

I turned my attention back to the screen. I had been taught that Neil Armstrong had taken several days to reach the moon. Surya Devta took only half a minute to land up in Kunti's room; that too, he didn't even need a rocket—he had simply walked. Science and Sanskrit had always appeared contradicting subjects to me at school.

For some reason, Surya Devta looked duller in comparison to the other gods in *Mahabharat*. He lacked the necessary confidence and didn't carry the hint of a smile that every other god did. When I look back, I suspect that his headgear had probably not been of the right size, making him look really uncomfortable in his mukut.

Kunti joined her hands and bowed in front of him, after which they talked some more. Surya Devta asked Kunti the purpose of her calling him. Kunti mentioned that she was simply testing her powers of summoning him and didn't have any purpose in mind. Surya Devta appeared visibly offended and said that he couldn't go back without giving her anything, so he would bless her with a baby. That was all he said—but no one in this world would have been as curious as I was to see the rest of the episode!

My eyes were glued on to the TV set. I looked at the wall clock. Only fifteen minutes of the show were left! I wondered if the act of producing the baby could be completed in those fifteen minutes. I had my fingers crossed.

But then, Kunti went mad. As Surya Devta insisted on giving her a baby, she started refusing his offer. Surya Devta told her that there was no going back, once he had uttered the blessing from his own mouth. But Kunti was still trying to resist.

'Have it, goddamnit!' I shouted at the TV, kicking up my legs on the chair.

Mom looked at me with surprise.

The world around me ceased to exist. The only existing entity was our Konark Rohini Deluxe 14-inch, black-and-white TV set, with Kunti and Surya Devta in it. Time was racing on the clock on the wall. I was so close to discovering the ultimate truth of my life—but Kunti was busy throwing her tantrums!

Exactly at 9.53 a.m., Surya Devta raised his right hand. A spectrum of flashing rays of light erupted from the centre of his stretched palm and alighted on Kunti's stomach, and then spread to engulf her entire body. The background music was that of a thunderstorm and soon the entire TV screen was drenched in light. All this while, I was so engrossed in it that I could almost feel the baby taking birth in my own tummy.

At 9.55 a.m., the rays dispersed. Surya Devta had done his job. Kunti had a baby boy in her arms. She didn't look happy.

I was very happy! I had seen it all. There wasn't any doubt left in my mind. I had seen it all, right from scratch. That was such a glorious end to my three-week-old dilemma and the most difficult puzzle of my life.

Some discoveries are worth remembering for a lifetime. Some discoveries are so close to the heart that only the discoverer can feel them and cherish them. I could empathize with my childhood hero Columbus. I felt exactly the way he might have felt after discovering America.

It was indeed a very happy Sunday. In the night, after a long time, I slept peacefully.

Early the next morning, I woke up feeling quite rested and energized. I felt as if I had achieved something in life.

Barefoot, in my vest and shorts and with a toothbrush in my mouth, I was roaming in our courtyard with an air of superiority. The white froth of the toothpaste was all over my mouth and some of it had dripped on to my vest as well.

Then, suddenly, one of our neighbours opened her window. We knew this lady well—she came to our house often to meet my mother. When I looked at her, I wanted to wish her a good morning, but I was afraid that all the froth in my mouth would spill out. She too saw me, but didn't say anything. She was busy doing something.

In the background, I heard my mother shouting at me. Often, when I brushed my teeth, I would forget to scrub all my teeth properly and go into a world of daydreaming, with the toothbrush stuck in my mouth. It was a usual thing for Mom to remind me to clean my upper teeth properly. On hearing her voice, I changed the direction of my brush from the left side of my mouth to the right. And then, all of a sudden, something caught my eye and my mouth fell open.

The neighbouring Aunty had stretched her arms outside of her window. In her hands was a spherical water vessel of the same kind I had seen in *Mahabharat*. *Oh boy!* I thought, and hid behind the guava tree in our garden for a better and unobstructed view. The brush was frozen in my mouth. I ignored Mom's instructions.

Aunty looked at the sun, mumbled something and started pouring water to the ground. I rubbed one leg against the other to drive away the garden flies. Her eyes were closed but her lips were moving. I tried to read that mantra she might have been reciting like Kunti but failed to do so, yet again.

The peppermint-flavoured froth on my lips stretched into the widest smile ever. The toothbrush slipped out of the gap formed after the loss of my two front teeth. My dry eyes twinkled. I looked at the sun and I looked at her. And I looked at the sun again, waiting to see the god walk down.

It would happen any time now!

'You don't want to go to the school or what?' My mother's sharp tone broke into my reverie.

She was standing right next to me. Then she began to drag me away.

'Mommy . . . Mommy . . . ik minute . . . oho . . . please . . . ik minute . . . pleaaaaase!' I begged, but it was an effort in vain.

She dragged me straightaway to the bathroom and warned, 'Five minutes and you should be through with your bath!'

I hated her and wanted to tell her that I knew she had lied to me. That she knew how I had been born. But for some reason, I couldn't do anything but stare at her eyes.

The cool water washed away my anger. By the time I was done with my bath, I had forgotten that I had been angry with Mom. But the thoughts of what must have happened to Aunty were still there.

After a while, when Mom was combing my hair and pulling it into a bun, she affectionately asked me, 'Kinnu dekh reha si bahar brush karde hoye?' [Whom were you looking at while you were brushing?]

I smiled but didn't answer.

She hung my schoolbag on my shoulders and asked again, 'Bol?'

'Woh teen number-vaali Aunty hai na . . .'

'Hmm . . .'

'. . . I saw her trying to have a baby,' I said confidently.

My mother froze for a moment and grabbed my shoulders tightly. She kneeled down to make eye contact with me.

There was a smile on her lips.

There was confusion in between the lines of her forehead.

~

Four years had passed by since I had been put into school. The first two years went by simply in setting the context and understanding what it meant to be the first in the class. The third year involved figuring out a way to achieve that. The fourth year—and the worst of all four—just proved that the previous years' answers were all wrong.

I was extremely happy that the final exams were over. And, right ahead of me, were the long summer vacations. But my parents were not as happy as I was, because I had failed to make them proud! They picked up my mark sheet and went through it a lot more times than I had held it in my own hands. I had scored well, but, according to them, not well enough to merit a pat on my back.

I had secured the tenth position in the class. We were some thirty-odd students, in all.

'See, this is where you need to focus,' Mom told me, pointing to the mathematics score on the mark sheet.

'If you can get all the answers right, this is one subject in which you can easily score 100 out of 100!' she said.

I had a score of 85 out of 100, and wondered whether another 15 marks would have made me the class topper. Mom explained that if I studied harder, there was nothing I couldn't achieve.

'Look at your classmate Mandeep. He had scored 100 out of 100. And he is far ahead of you! You should be friends with him at school,' Mom said, before she headed for the kitchen.

Back in my room, I kept thinking about the twenty other students who were behind me in this race. I wondered if their mothers wanted them to be friends with me . . .

But I did listen to my mother. I didn't want to disappoint her. So, updating my friends' circle was the very first change I made. Personally, I have never understood this practice of making and breaking friendships based on people's mark sheets. Didn't we make friends by choosing the people we got along the best with? However, there was something more to it this time. Irrespective of whether Mom was right or wrong, her comparing me to Mandeep had only made me more jealous of him.

8

I Have a Pen!

It was when I got to Class VI that I started feeling truly mature. I think it had to do with two major changes in my life.

First, an ink pen had replaced my pencil. It made a big difference when I felt its presence—in my hands, in my pencil box and in my shirt's pocket.

I remember how obsessed I used to be with my ink pen. I loved its nib, and that, to me, was the most beautiful part of the pen. In my free time, it was quite normal for me to keep staring at the nib of my pen and wonder how that thing was so nicely carved at the corners. I would be amazed to observe how that chiselled semi-cylinder of metal ended in such a sharp, pointed tip. However, the most beautiful aspect of the pen for me was to watch how, right through the centre of its shiny exterior, a super-fine channel of ink flowed and took the shape of letters on paper.

It was love at first sight!

I would spend about fifteen to twenty minutes every night checking the level of ink left in my pen and refilling it with a dropper. At the end of my refilling exercise, I would seal the lid of my Chelpark ink bottle and then wipe the extra ink off the outer surface of the pen, especially the surface of the nib around the thick ink channel. I wanted the nib to be as clean and shiny as possible. If there was ever a leakage, I would rub the pen against my hair. I had learnt doing that from my tuition sir.

If ever there was a point in time when I felt grown up, this was it. And with my growing up, I also started expecting other grown-up privileges. I remember, one day, before the pen had made its entry into my life, while I was doing my science homework of fill-in-the-blanks for a lesson called 'Healthy Breakfast', I had asked my mother, 'Why do I have to drink only milk? Why can't I drink tea, like you?'

'Because you are a kid,' came the reply. 'And tea isn't good for kids. When you grow up, you can start having tea.'

Busy sharpening my pencil, I thought about what she had said. 'So when will I be a grown-up?'

Mom looked at me and then at the pencil that I had been sharpening. She answered, 'The day you will start writing with a pen.' And she had smiled.

Since that day, I had started associating the use of a pen

with the status of being a grown-up. I had been waiting for a long time to get into Class VI, because that's when, according to our curriculum, we were supposed to start writing with pens. And when I did get into Class VI, I claimed my licence to drink tea!

The second major milestone of growing up for me was to become the proud owner of a bicycle. Getting the bicycle wasn't easy. I had long craved for it and had been demanding it for years. Time and again I used to bring up the subject of my would-be bicycle, and time and again I was denied one.

'Tu haaley chhota hai, cycle chalaan vaastey,' [You are still too young to ride a bicycle] Mom had said one day when I had initiated the topic.

'Par Devesh hor Mandeep vi chhotey hain. Ohna kol cycle hai,' [But Devesh and Mandeep are young as well. They have bicycles] I argued.

'What about Anju, Meenu, Rashmi?' Mom countered.

'Mom, they are girls!' I tried to bring in the gender difference for my benefit.

But my mother wasn't going to retreat. She threw a few boys' names at me, who she knew did not have a bicycle. I wanted to get back at her, and I even had a very reasonable argument, but for some reason I couldn't say that to her face. Knowing it wouldn't hold, I didn't debate the subject further.

I expressed my annoyance by not talking to her that evening. However, in a short while, Mom began to serve food to my brother and me. While Tinku ate his food, I kept staring at it blankly. I was hungry, but on the outside I was putting up a non-violent act of protest. Mom was still in the kitchen, making a few chapattis for Dad.

At first, I was determined not to eat unless Mom agreed to buy me a bicycle. A little later, when I felt hungrier, I resolved that I'd start eating as soon as Mom shouted at me for not eating. That was the point to which I would stretch my ego.

But nothing of the sort happened. Being in the kitchen, Mom wasn't even aware that I wasn't eating. Hence she didn't shout.

Soon emotion and hunger acted in unison and broke me down. And that's when my eyes turned moist. Gradually, through wet eyelashes, the food in front of me became blurred. Tinku looked at me. I looked back at him. Seeing me in that condition made him somewhat confused. He got off his chair and went to the kitchen. The very thought of my little brother telling my mother about my crying, which would make Mom come running to console and feed me, made me comfortable.

But I was wrong. All my little unsympathetic brother did was to return with some more dal for himself. Then he climbed back into his chair with his legs hanging in the air, holding a spoon which he had still not learnt to hold properly. He watched me sobbing as if nothing had happened. He was hopeless!

I will never share my bicycle with you, I thought to myself while giving him the most disgusting look ever. Even that didn't seem to have any effect on him.

And while I was thinking about him, I forgot about crying.

Mom called out from the kitchen, asking me if I wanted more chapatti. I didn't respond. She called out again. I still didn't respond.

Finally, she came to the living room, only to see my food untouched. She saw me crying silently. Worried to see me that way, she ran towards me and took my hand.

'Ki hogaya, beta?' [What's the matter, son?] she asked, worried.

I didn't say anything, but wrapped my arms around her. And that's when I gave way to my feelings. I started crying loudly, because I could not bear to be angry any more. My non-violent protest got washed away in a flood of tears. A little later, Mom fed me with her hands. I felt cared for. As she fed me every bite, she explained to me that I had grown up enough and that I should understand our family's financial condition. She offered me some water and, after I had taken a sip, she told me that I should not make demands for everything I wanted. All this while, as she kept talking to me and made me finish my dinner, I kept holding her chunni in my hands, feeling disappointed by her explanations.

That night, lying in my bed, I thought of how I had wanted to respond to my mother when she had pointed out the boys in my class who didn't come to school on bicycles. I wanted to tell her that those boys didn't even need a bike—their dads had scooters. Every day, they would be dropped off to school on their scooters. It was embarrassing for me that my father didn't possess one.

And from that embarrassment came hate—I hated my father because he wasn't a doctor or an engineer like my friends' fathers. Just like the other boys of my class, I too wanted to stand in between my dad's legs when he would drive a scooter. Like them, I too wanted to press the horn and make the world get out of my way. Like them, I too wanted to let my classmates know that my father had dropped me off to school on his scooter. But I knew my father couldn't afford one, and so I was only asking for a bicycle.

In the afternoon, when school got over, my friends would go back home in those nice box-shaped six-seater school rickshaws. Their dads would be busy at work and therefore couldn't turn up at school to pick them up. So they all enjoyed a leisurely rickshaw ride, where they chatted with each other and watched the world go by. They would all hang their water bottles down the rear grill and get into the rickshaw, after which the rickshaw puller would lock the door. From inside the rickshaw, they all would look out and wave their hands out of those square windows, bidding goodbye to the others. There were scores of rickshaws leaving from the school in the afternoon, and I would watch them all going away. All this while I would keep holding my brother's hand, waiting for Dad to arrive on his bicycle to take us back home.

Once, my classmate Sourav had asked me, 'Tum hamaarey saath rickshaw mein kyun nahi aatey ho?' [Why don't you come along with us in the rickshaw?]

'Mere Daddy bolte hain rickshaw-vaaley late kar dete hain. Hum cycle pe jaldi ghar pahonch jaatey hain.' [My Dad says rickshaws are usually late. We can reach home faster on his bicycle.]

That day, I asked Dad to pedal his bicycle faster and beat Sourav's rickshaw, so that I could prove to him that I was right. But, deep inside, I was aware of the truth. The rickshaw puller charged a hundred rupees per month per child. Our father couldn't have afforded a monthly rickshaw service for the two of us.

Therefore, all I had asked for was a bicycle. But Mom, while serving me food that night, had advised me to postpone this demand. I recalled my mother's words—I should understand our family's financial condition and should not be demanding. I kept thinking about it over and over again. I don't remember when sleep took over me . . .

. . . And, the next morning was one of the best mornings of my life! I was riding my bicycle to school. I had hung my water bottle across the bicycle bell on the right side of the handle. My schoolbag was safely tucked in the carrier behind me. I was the happiest kid in town and wasn't able to contain my smile. On my way to school, I overtook some of my friends on their dads' scooters and a few in those box-shaped rickshaws. Then I turned naughty—I showed off my favourite stunt of letting go of the handle and pedalling the bicycle faster. I was my own hero!

But I wanted to be everyone else's hero as well. So I raced my bicycle into the school complex, leaving behind me a trail of wind and dust. I pushed up from my seat and pedalled the bicycle hard and fast—like no one had ever seen before! Without any hassle, I raced my bicycle all the way up the tall staircase. The crowd applauded. A lot of girls were cheering my name—'Ravinder! Ravinder!' Acknowledging them with a passing smile, I raised the front wheel of my bicycle on to the railing of the staircase. My next stunt was going to be to apply a quick brake and bring the bicycle to a skidding halt just at the precipice of the staircase.

Exactly at that moment, I heard my mother call out: 'Utth jaa, hun! School jaana hai.' [Wake up! You've to go to school.]

And it was all over. I was back in bed, in my daily vest and pajamas.

On my way to school, while my father pedalled his bicycle, I asked him, 'Ik gall puchhan, Daddy?' [May I ask you something, Daddy?]

'Puchh?' he answered, without paying me much attention.

'Tussi mainnu cycle le dogey ki?' [Will you get me a bicycle?]

~

The unfulfilled desire for a bicycle had not dampened my competitive spirit at school. By the end of Class VI, I was very close to being declared the winning rat. But Hindi turned out to be my weak link. Just 5 more marks, and I would have been able to make my parents proud.

I had worked very hard this time.

Interestingly, and quite contrary to my expectations, my parents were a lot happier this time. However, *I* wasn't happy. Blame it on the competitiveness that had, by then, so badly become a part of my mental structure, but I failed to be happy despite coming second in my entire class.

I only realized this when my parents smiled, on looking at my mark sheet. I reminded them that I hadn't come first.

Yet, Mom patted me on the back and so did Dad. That made me feel good about myself. Even though I wasn't happy with my results, I was happy because my parents were finally happy.

Being inches close to your goal may have any one of these two impacts on your mind—one, you grow complacent at the thought that you've *almost* reached your goal and will soon get there quite easily; or else, that you work harder to sustain your current position, while making calculated progress towards the final goal. My parents were believers in the second impact. Unfortunately, *I* belonged to the first school of thought—that I would easily make it to the top sooner or later.

But that year, as per my mother's wishes, studying my

curriculum for Class VII did not wait till the school reopened after the vacation; it began right in the middle of the summer vacations! While I stayed at home, I was made to go through the entire *Baal Bharati*—the Hindi literature textbook—and *Vyaakaran*, the Hindi grammar textbook.

I enjoyed reading the stories in *Baal Bharati*, but the ghost of *Vyaakaran* just flew over my head. And because I believed in being complacent, I decided to take Hindi less seriously when the books were later being taught in class.

Big mistake!

By the time I realized how seriously it was going to affect my results, it was already too late. Within seven months of getting a pat on my back from my parents, I once again became the reason behind their sadness and frustration.

No, I didn't do badly in my final exams. The finals were still a few months away. But I did very badly in my half-yearly exams. From the second position, I slipped down to the seventh—in a matter of seven months!

I remember how I delayed revealing my marks to my parents. I could not escape it, for the test papers had to be signed by my parents and returned to school. At one point, I even planned to sign them on my own, but stopped myself from doing so at the last moment.

Those few days, I lived in the terror of receiving my parents' scolding. And, the very next week, my fears came true. There was a parent–teacher meeting in school. Despite all my efforts to manoeuvre my mother away from the

Hindi teacher, the inevitable happened. The rest of my week turned into a disaster zone.

'No more playing in the evening. Get up early in the morning and study!' Mom instructed me strictly, after I came back from school.

It felt like a social boycott. My playtime was reduced from two hours to just one. Everything I wished for in life was now connected with my results. 'You will only get your bicycle when you study hard and get good results.' *What? People who didn't score top marks didn't ride bicycles?*

I was still the same boy who had done wonderfully in the last final exams and made his parents proud. And they were the same parents who had patted their son on his back. How come, then, that our relationship had suddenly come to this? After a point, I started losing all my self-confidence. I felt I was good for nothing. The fact that I was still better than at least twenty students in my class failed to hold up my spirits.

My father, who, only till a week before had believed that I would make him proud, started openly lamenting that his dream might never come true. And, to add to my misery, the *Chitrahaar* music programme started airing this new song twice a week on Doordarshan, with lyrics that went: *Papa kehte hain bada naam karega . . . Beta hamaara aisa kaam karega* . . . Talk about wrong timing, man!

Again, the race to do better brought about one more change for me. At the parent–teacher meeting, my class teacher and my mother mutually agreed to the Hindi teacher's proposal of shifting me to the first bench in the class. All three of them believed that it would have a positive effect on my concentration levels.

I wondered—with that logic, should there be any benches in the classroom from the second row onwards at all?

9

A Change of Schools

'No! I don't want to go to that school!' I screamed.

'Chup kar ja, hun,' Mom warned me. She did not want me to make a fuss about it, and so asked me to shut up.

'But why are you doing this to me?' I retorted in anger.

'Because you have cleared the entrance exam for this school and now you will have to join it,' she answered in a voice that was louder and sterner.

I got scared and counter-questioned her, but this time in a lower voice, 'But I have cleared the entrance exam of Madnawati as well! Why aren't you sending me to that school?'

She didn't respond and went back to chopping onions in the kitchen. I walked out to the veranda, as a mark of my silent protest. I sat there and sulked for a while.

The school in Burla conducted classes only till Class VII. Of course, it was a small institution. Even the state-board-affiliated coaching centre had more students than we had in our class! But as this was the only English-medium school in Burla, to continue further studies in the same board, one had to move to Sambalpur, the nearest city as well as the district headquarters. And I had successfully passed Class VII. So the argument I was having with my mother was about which school I should go to next.

There were quite a few English-medium schools in Sambalpur. Three out of the four that I knew about were affiliated to CBSE (the Central Board of Secondary Education), while the convent school was affiliated to ICSE (Indian Certificate of Secondary Education).

I had a vested interest in joining the convent school. It was really quite simple—the girls of that school wore skirts as part of their school uniform! On my way to school in Burla, I had seen the bare legs of a few girls while they hopped on to their school buses in the mornings. From the boys of that school, I had heard secret stories of them intentionally dropping the pencil to the floor, in order to get a peek into the mysterious territory lying between the legs of the girls behind their benches. Those early-morning eye candies and motivating stories from the boys had made me daydream of some day joining the convent school.

But my daydream of becoming the one to drop the pencil and have fun got busted for two reasons. Firstly, the convent was the most expensive school in the city. I came to know of how expensive it was from Nishant, a good friend of mine who went to the same convent school. That day, he was narrating yet another motivating story, about a girl who sat on the bench next to him, on the left, and preferred to roll down her socks and pull up her skirt as soon as she entered the school campus.

The moment I learnt that, I questioned him about the expenses of studying at that school. 'Convent school mein padhne ke liye kitne paise dene honge?'

'I pay two hundred and fifty as my monthly fee, and the bus fare is another hundred bucks,' Nishant answered after doing the math.

'What?! Three hundred and fifty rupees!!!' It was as if he had dropped a grenade.

For someone whose father was paying seventy rupees per month in Burla, it was nothing short of a grenade. Right then, it was clear in my mind that my father wouldn't be able to afford a school with girls in skirts for his son.

Secondly, the convent school taught only till Class X, whereas the CBSE schools went on till Class XII. One would have to change schools again after the tenth. There was no point in changing schools again after three years. My dream was dying a natural death.

I thought about the girls in all the three CBSE-affiliated schools who wore boring salwar–kameezes with chunnis. *Nothing exciting there!* As far as this criterion was concerned, the other three schools stood equally disqualified. So my task at hand was to choose one among the disqualified ones.

Keeping aside the girls' uniform, Madnawati was the most happening of the three CBSE schools. They had a school bus that came all the way up to Burla. The Central School had a decent school complex, but its quality of education was the lowest among the three. The Guru Nanak Public School was a smaller institution in comparison, with an average quality of education. It also didn't have the school-bus facility to Burla, which is why hardly anyone from Burla joined that school.

My second choice became Madnawati, because all my classmates from the previous school were opting for Madnawati. But my parents were forcing me to join GNPS. I knew that both schools were far away from my home. I knew that everything would be different—the school, the classmates, the teachers and everything else. But, amid all these differences, I would have felt comfortable having my old classmates around me; whereas at GNPS I would be all alone! While all of them would comfortably go to school and come back in their school bus, I would be deprived of this fun. I would have to do my daily up and down in the public buses.

With all these concerns, I had been arguing with my parents. But at that age, I didn't have the guts to go against my parents' will.

Two days before joining GNPS, I overheard a conversation

between my mother and my father. It was then that I found the reason behind Dad's adamant decision to admit me to that school and Mom's lack of support for my stand.

It was night and I was lying on my bed with my eyes closed. Dad had come home quite late and Mom had to serve him dinner. They thought I was fast asleep and, therefore, began chatting quite openly with each other.

'Odey saarey dost Madnawati jaa rahe hain. Mainu pata hai odey wastey mushkil hovega.' [All his friends are going to join Madnawati. I know it is going to be difficult for him.] This was Mom, speaking as she sat next to Dad while he ate.

A pause. Then, he said, 'Thoda time lagega. Phir sab thik ho jaayega. Hor koi rasta vi nahi hai saddey kol.' [It will take some time. Then everything will be fine. We don't have any other way out.] I guessed that they were both looking at me as they were talking.

I made sure I didn't open my eyes. I needed to know their thoughts.

I learnt that it was financially difficult for my parents to admit me to any of the other schools in Sambalpur. The fees were high and the daily travel to Sambalpur was going to pinch my dad's pocket hard. But they didn't want to leave any stone unturned in securing a good senior school for me.

GNPS was a ray of hope for them. The school was governed by a Sikh management committee. Dad had put an application in front of the committee, mentioning the financial condition of our family. Based on it, he had pleaded in that application to exempt me from paying the school fee.

Given the fact that Dad was a priest in a gurdwara, and also taking our family's background into consideration, the committee—after holding multiple rounds of talks—had approved the application. That would save Dad one hundred and fifty rupees a month, which was the school fee. In those days, this was a good amount of money to be saved.

The moment I came to know the reason behind my parents' decision, I let go of my anguish and prepared myself to embrace GNPS as my next school.

As expected, the ride to my new school turned out to be a difficult ball game. To reach the school was an ordeal by itself. The bus stand was a kilometre away from my home. On my first day at the new school, Dad had given me a ride on his bicycle till the bus stand. He had coordinated the timing of our getting to the bus stop with that of one of our neighbours, who used go to Sambalpur for work every day. I had never travelled alone in public buses, so Dad thought it would be good to have someone to be with me on the bus, at least for the initial few days.

Rammi Uncle, our neighbour, was right on time. The bus stop where I had to get off was a forty-five-minute journey away. When we started the journey, Rammi Uncle told me that on that day he would not be able to get down at my stop and accompany me to school, since he had some urgent personal work and would have to travel till the last stop. I wasn't sure if he had mentioned this to Dad when he promised to take care of me. Instead, he told me which road to follow in order to reach my school.

I was a little scared to be left all alone in an unfamiliar place. I got off at my stop and walked along the road that Rammi Uncle had pointed out to me from the window of the bus. The place was an industrial area with lots of trucks and lorries running down the road. The street I had to take was dirty. It was littered with paper and dirty polybags. It was crowded too. There were a number of vendors selling breakfast on their open carts and a lot of rickshaw pullers and truck drivers eating their first meal of the day. Stray dogs and pigs dominated one corner that was full of mud and stagnant water, swarming with flies and mosquitoes. The foul smell of it all overpowered my nostrils.

Amid all this, I made sure that my new white shirt and new water bottle didn't get spoiled.

After a short walk, I came across multiple turns on the same street, and realized that Rammi Uncle hadn't told me about those. So I had to take the advice of the local rickshaw pullers to find my way. To make some easy money, the rickshaw pullers offered me a ride to school. I refused them and only borrowed their advice, which came for free. Most of them suggested a well-known shortcut which led through a barren rice field. It was a route meant only for pedestrians. There was no way one could ride any vehicle through it.

I followed the lane. Soon enough, I passed by a very tiny slum. Some fifty more steps ahead, I found myself at the edge of a vast field. It was barren except for wild shrubs that grew here and there. About a mile ahead, I could see a few trucks parked on the road on the other side. They were dumping soil on to the field.

A signboard ahead of me read: 'Railway Colony'. It looked like the entire field was being converted into a residential colony. The board marked the boundary of the land that the railways had acquired, and, right there, the land ahead of me was elevated. At a distance, on the edge of that raised land, I saw a few people squatting and defaecating in the open. They didn't feel the need to either hide their butts or their faces. I guessed they must have been from the slum that I had left behind me.

I had to climb up a pile of field soil about eight feet high. I continued to walk along what appeared to be a small kaccha path within the field. The lack of greenery on that narrow lane made me assume that people must be using it quite often—which was why, unlike the rest of the field, it wasn't overgrown with wild grass. After great difficulty and more than one and a half kilometres of walking, I finally reached my school.

I was familiar with the school complex as I had visited it a couple of times earlier—once during the entrance exam and twice for the application that Dad had to submit to the school committee. But I wasn't sure where my classroom was, so I made my way straight to the principal's room. I'm quite sure I was probably one of the rare students who thought of meeting the principal in the very first hour of their very first day at school!

He was a Sikh. I had seen him multiple times in the Sambalpur gurdwara. I used to wish him Sat Sri Akal whenever I came across him in the gurdwara.

As I walked to his office, I was confused whether I should wish him, 'Sat Sri Akal, Uncle' or 'Good morning, Sir.' But I needn't have worried. Thank God, the principal was not in his office yet. But his peon was on time. So I approached him and asked if he would escort me to my classroom. In his khaki uniform, he was basking on a stool outside the principal's office.

'Bhaiya, class tak chodd dogey?' I asked him politely.

He looked like a buffalo grazing in the fields to me—the same lazy, careless actions and the same complacent mood. He was also chewing something, completing the picture of a buffalo in my mind. He gave me a blank look, and then his head swung back to its earlier position. He had ignored me. How could I tolerate someone ignoring me! I threatened to report him to the principal, whom my father knew.

A few minutes later, I was walking down the centre of the school complex, with the Buffalo Man carrying my bag and water bottle. He left me at the entrance of my new classroom. He didn't talk, and only made a hand gesture towards it. I guess even that was too much for me to expect from him.

The class had already started and, seeing me, all the students turned towards the door. Finding her students distracted, the class teacher also looked at the door and spotted me. Suddenly I felt embarrassed.

The class teacher, the only person who had been talking so far in the class, fell silent. The students, who had been listening to the teacher, started talking among themselves.

'Yes?' the teacher asked me from a distance. She looked at me over her spectacles, which rested almost on the tip of her nose.

'Aaaa! . . . Aa . . . Ma'am, I am Ravinder,' I managed to say hesitantly.

She quickly glanced at the attendance register and said, 'Oh yes, Ravinder!'

She walked up to me. 'So you are late on your very first day in this school!'

I was ashamed of myself. 'Ma'am, I live in Burla. I didn't know the way to the school,' I defended myself.

She smiled and said warmly, 'Come in. I will mark you "present" in the attendance register. And now that you know the way, don't be late again. All right?'

'Yes, Ma'am,' I said and happily stepped inside the class—but I stopped right there! Right in front of me were my new classmates, who had been exchanging whispers and smiles among themselves ever since I had arrived. After I had stepped in, those whispers and smiles had become louder.

'Haww! Look at him,' I heard from one corner of the

class, and the whispers spread till they had reached the other corner. I felt mortified. Reaching late had been a mistake! I became nervous. I felt as if my legs had turned to jelly and I could not move. If I could just get a seat, I would sit down quickly and this embarrassment would end. I looked around for one, but, in my nervousness, I couldn't find any. I simply stood at the entrance with my schoolbag on my shoulders, a water bottle in my hand and my legs shaking.

Then I suddenly overheard the word: 'Half-pant!' That was followed by a round of giggles on my right.

And that's when I realized the blunder. I looked at the boys in the first row, then in the second and then at everyone in totality. All of them wore full navy-blue pants!

There was only one person who was in half-pants—me.

I looked to my right. The girls had their legs covered demurely in salwars. The teacher wore a sari. So I was the only one brandishing my naked legs in the half-pants that barely reached down my thighs!

Not only was I the only boy who had offered a detailed view of his legs in the full public gaze of the class, but I guessed I was also the only one in the entire school to do so—because, in that moment of nervousness, I realized that even the Buffalo Man was wearing full pants!

Oh God! What do I do now? I thought to myself. A sense of heavy shame bore down my back.

In my mind, even the half-pants I was wearing had fallen off. All of a sudden, I felt vulnerable to these people whom I had never known.

I wished to undo that moment. I wished to run back and out of the school. I wished to board the first bus back to Burla. I wished to hide myself in my bed at home.

But if wishes were horses . . .

In my previous school, it was all right to wear half-pants. I wasn't aware that an upgrade in schools had to come along with an upgrade of my pants as well. I had become the butt of many a joke for the entire class on Day One itself.

'There! Go there and sit next to Sushil,' the teacher pointed towards a vacant seat in the last row, the rest of which was occupied by girls.

It was my ill fate that, out of all the seats in the class, I was asked to go sit in the one for which I had to walk down the aisle dominated by girls. How badly did I want a seat on the other side of the classroom, where most of the boys were seated! I looked for one but, again, found none of them empty.

'What happened?' the class teacher asked.

'No, Ma'am, nothing,' I replied and looked at the seat that she had pointed me to.

I filled my lungs with a deep breath, and took my first steps to embrace whatever was left of my public humiliation. I walked through the territory of giggling female faces—curious eyes scanning my hairy thighs. I avoided any sort of eye contact. I wanted to look more confident, as if I didn't know what they were talking about. But my body language was not in sync with my mind and, all that while, my hands reached down to pull my half-pants down to my knees, hiding as much of myself as possible. I walked like a lame duck in a pond of female crocodiles. As I progressed along my path, I felt all heads turn towards me.

I heaved a sigh of relief when I finally reached the desk at which I was supposed to sit.

Sushil picked up his notebook from my side of the table. I gave him a smile. He continued to smile. I pulled out my handkerchief from my pocket and wiped the sweat from my forehead.

The class continued to stare at me till the class teacher announced, 'All right, class, so where were we?'

Ma'am resumed the lesson. The heads turned back to their respective books, and only intermittently did they get back to me. I sat with my schoolbag on my lap, so that it would cover my thighs. I didn't want the period to end. I didn't want the boys and girls to discuss me in the open and aloud when the teacher was gone.

But then, that period ended. The teacher left. And I became the talk of the school.

I didn't go to school for the next two days.

That was the time that the tailor in Burla had taken to sew my new navy-blue full pants.

10

The Power of Chapter 10

More than half of the curriculum of Class IX had been covered. Winter had set in nicely. The red-coloured school sweaters were out of the trunks and on us, brightening the otherwise bland navy-blue-and-white colour combination of the school uniform. The ones that had been pulled out of the trunk very recently, and not yet put out in the sun, smelled of naphthalene balls.

To get out of bed early in the morning had become challenging. And this challenge had led to a significant drop in the school's attendance. Every day there were a few students who would skip class—if not for the entire day, then definitely the first period. This kind of absence from the class required the student to submit a leave or a late-coming application. Interestingly, none of the leave applications would mention the real reason, i.e., the student was too lazy to wake up on chilly mornings!

While one leave application might have narrated a kind-hearted story of saving a stray puppy from dying on the road, another might describe in detail how the chain of the bicycle had slipped out of the wheel. Most of us were smart enough to write applications with new and unique reasons for being late, but there was a bunch of students who defined the heights of laziness. They were too lazy to even change their 'reasons for being late' in their subsequent applications.

Gurpreet, who sat next to me in the left row and seldom took baths on winter mornings, would simply change the animal that she claimed to have saved! At first it was a puppy, then a kitten, followed by a goat. I thought given the rate at which she was using up different animals to rescue herself, she would have been left with nothing but elephants and horses by the end of winter.

When, for the fourth time, Nandu blamed the faulty chain of his bicycle for his coming late to school, the class teacher asked, 'Why don't you think of changing your bicycle, Nandu?' and the class broke into a laugh. Nandu, too, shamelessly joined in the laughter, least bothered that his lie had been caught!

There also used to be a few cunning minds who believed that they must keep their reasons exclusive. This bunch of students invested almost half the night in thinking up one great excuse. That was precisely why, I think, half the time they used to wake up late! At school, these kids would keep their applications highly guarded, so that no one would find out and reuse their exclusive reasons.

So, the ritual of arriving late to school continued. And so did the ritual of submitting fake applications. Amid all this, there used to be some genuine cases as well. But then, it was pointless to try to prove that your application for leave was genuine.

Then, one day, our class made history. We recorded full attendance—for the very first time that winter.

This was not a random happening. There was a reason behind this historical achievement.

This was a Friday and the first subject of the day was Biology. Having survived the boring section about the plant kingdom, we had arrived at the chapters on the animal kingdom. And, on that day, we were about to start 'Chapter 10—Reproduction'.

Ever since we had bought our books at the beginning of the term, the Bio book was the one whose pages had been flipped through the most. And it was *this* chapter that we had all flipped through the pages for. Time and again at home, in privacy, I would open this book and stop at this chapter on the page where a man and a woman stood, pictured naked. I didn't believe my eyes when, for the first time, I came across this page. I wondered how something of that sort could exist in a schoolbook. It was my first experience of seeing lifelike sketches of a man and woman without clothes on—and it was quite shocking. In spite of the fact that it was my schoolbook, I was worried about what my parents would think of me if they got to know that this was what I was studying in my school. Therefore, I used to place that book right at the bottom of the stack of my schoolbooks in the shelf, making it as inaccessible as possible for them.

So, on that exciting morning, after the prayer, unlike the other days when the students would disperse to drink water or to go to the loo before the first period started, everyone headed straight for the classroom. And then we separated into two groups—boys and girls.

There was much excitement and whispering in the class, especially in the back benches, where a few of us had started making naughty jokes. The whispers were followed by raucous laughter from the boys' side, while the girls looked silently on, either ignoring us or giving us dirty looks. They wanted to make us feel as if we were unnecessarily excited about certain things that were quite normal. But we knew that, deep inside, they were equally excited. What double standards!

The necessity of being able to talk about human private parts in public had given rise to code words. Creativity and imagination were at their peak when we replaced all the biological names of body parts on the naked man and woman in Chapter 10 with the names of fruits that had a close resemblance to each particular body part. Suddenly, that page looked like a fruit shop. In the end, we even gave names to the man and the woman. We called them 'Chintu' and 'Babli', after popular names in our town.

The madness continued. Some enterprising souls drew the figures from scratch on the last page of their notebooks, then tore off those pages and passed them on to others for review. I, too, was one of these people. When my paper landed in Sushil's hands, he looked at the drawing and shouted appreciatively, 'Oh, beta! Gazab banaaya hai be tu toh!' [Hey, dude! Great job you have done!]

Right then my eyes fell on Bhavna, whose eyes were following me all this time. Now, I had a soft corner for Bhavna and had always treated her like my sister. She was looking at me with disgust and then she said out loud, 'Tu bhi unki tarah ban gaya hai na, Ravinder?' [You too have become like those people, haven't you, Ravinder?]

I couldn't say anything in reply. I stammered, and then I stopped myself. There was no explanation. But the feeling of guilt lasted only for a minute. I looked around—everyone other than me was busy celebrating the spirit of reading 'Reproduction'.

Then suddenly someone behind me announced, 'Nandu has got hold of the convent school's biology book. It has close-up visuals of the reproductive organs, something that is missing in our book!'

And I lost it. This was too much excitement to miss! I looked at the boys and then back at Bhavna. Half a minute back, I was wondering how to redeem myself in Bhavna's eyes. But having heard what the backbenchers had announced, my mind was immediately made up! I escaped Bhavna's glare, and, without bothering to respond to her question, ran back to the backbenchers. I tried to push my way in to treat my eyes to the close-up view. The book was snatched around from one hand to another. I'm not sure if anybody else managed to see the images very clearly, but I didn't.

Suddenly, all the commotion was interrupted. The loud laughter, the dirty jokes, the chatter—all died down in a second. Bio Ma'am had arrived. She took her time in coming though, listening to the chaos from outside the classroom, but choosing to keep quiet.

When the voices died down, she walked to her chair with grace, just as she always used to do. She was one of the most good-looking teachers in the school. She must have been somewhere in her mid-twenties. All of us knew that she wasn't yet married. She looked gorgeous in her maroon chudidaar–suit, paired with matching bangles and sandals. She took her chair and then opened the attendance register.

That day, every roll number she called was followed by either a 'Yes, Ma'am' or 'Present, Ma'am'. As she approached the last roll number, she had a sly smile on her face. Guess she had seen this phenomenon of cent per cent attendance in the previous years as well.

That was the power of Chapter 10!

As soon as she was through with the roll call, Bio Ma'am picked up the chalk. There was pin-drop silence. The boys were almost holding their breaths. Her sandals made a tick-tock sound as she walked to write on the blackboard that had been freshly scrubbed clean by the monitor of the class.

R–E–P–R–O–D–U–C–T–I–O–N

. . . she wrote in her stylish handwriting. Every letter of that word, along with the scratchy sound of the chalk on the blackboard, raised ripples of excitement within us. For the girls in our class, it seemed to be yet another chapter and they prepared themselves to take notes. For us boys, it was nothing less than the morning show of an adult movie—that too right after the morning prayers. We looked at each other and exchanged naughty smiles. The girls didn't dare to look anywhere and kept their eyes focused on the blackboard.

Bio Ma'am progressed with the lesson. Five minutes passed . . .

. . . then ten, twenty. And then thirty.

THIRTY MINUTES!!!

And nothing exciting happened. Absolutely nothing!

Disheartening as it was, our fantasies never saw the light of day. We wanted the teacher to talk about the vital body parts, but she was wandering somewhere inside the body, in between cells and zygotes. She had gone off on a different tangent altogether. We wanted to talk about the breathtaking visible process and actions of reproduction. She, for some reason, was just not coming out of explaining the boring invisible process of what happens inside. We wanted to skim the surface of the subject matter, but she was busy diving deep into it!

'When the X chromosome of the father meets the X chromosome of the mother, a girl is born,' she explained. Then she added, 'But when the Y chromosome of the father meets the X chromosome of the mother, a boy is born.'

She repeated that multiple times, and finally asked, 'And what does this show?'

She looked at the class from the left to the right, expecting some braveheart to answer that one. An uncomfortable silence descended upon the boys' half of the classroom, which felt cheated and was about to break down into tears.

'That you don't have anything interesting to teach,' Sushil whispered in frustration.

The boys around him giggled and brought him to everyone else's attention.

Sushil Aggarwal, a hard-core backbencher, was the most notorious guy in the class. There was no doubt about this tag, as it was the unanimous belief of our class, and Sushil too had accepted this fact. Girls hated him for his notorious behaviour; boys loved him for his guts and the fun he used to bring to the class. And, fortunately or unfortunately, he sat next to me.

'What's going on there?' Bio Ma'am raised the duster, pointing at us.

No one at the back responded. The most we did was to stop smiling.

The next moment, Archana, who was the topper of the class, grabbed Ma'am's attention by raising her hand to answer the question.

'Yes, Archana?' Ma'am asked her to speak.

'That means whether the baby is a boy or a girl has nothing do with the mother. It all depends on the father's chromosome.' She finished, and stood there waiting for Ma'am to praise her intelligence.

Which happened the very next moment. 'Very good, Archana! But uneducated people, especially in villages, blame the mother for the gender of their child. Now sit down.'

We found nothing interesting in this discovery.

'Hell, man! X and Y—here also? Bio ki class hai ki algebra ki?' Sushil cried out aloud, unable to hold back his frustration.

'Seriously, Sushil . . . Do something, man!' we encouraged him, trying to get some fun out of his madness.

So he raised his hand, interrupting the lecture. He said he had a question to ask—a rare act from him. We all waited.

'Yes, Sushil?' Ma'am gave him the permission to ask his question.

Sushil stood up, adjusted the belt of his trousers and tucked in his shirt. He tried to conceal his smile but could not; so he smiled on shamelessly. This gave the class an idea of the kind of question he was about to ask.

'Ma'am, how and when does father ka X meet mother ka X?'

A master stroke that was!

Sushil's courage in asking this was deeply admired by all of us. On the boys' side of the classroom, laughter erupted like a volcano. We tried hard to keep it down but that too felt like a challenge. The backbenchers celebrated this ultimate joke by tapping hard on the table.

In the girls' camp, whispers of 'Oh shit!' and 'Oh God!' were followed by embarrassed smiles. They were probably sympathizing with the teacher.

The only person who managed to hold her smile was Bio Ma'am. However, in order to bring the much-needed silence to class, she had to shout out: 'Silence!'

That only managed to silence half the class. She tapped the duster three times on the desk, until, gradually, the entire class came to a still. She had managed to handle the erupting chaos quite well. With that she regained some confidence, and went to answer Sushil's question.

Bio Ma'am looked right into his eyes. 'When the male sperm comes in contact with the female egg, that's when either X or Y from the male meets the X of female. Is that clear?' she asked sternly.

At that unexpected reply, Sushil couldn't even decide whether he should nod his head up and down or shake it left and right. So our hero landed up doing both. It was hilarious!

But as soon as Ma'am turned towards the blackboard, everyone turned towards Sushil. There was a smile on every face. We raised our hands to give him a thumbs-up sign. This was our admiration for him.

However, Sushil wasn't moved by our appreciation for him. He was still thinking over the interesting question he had asked and the boring answer that the teacher had countered it with.

He looked at us, rubbed his palm against his forehead in disappointment and said, 'Yeh kya bakwaas kare jaa rahi hai?'

Someone else in the back whispered, 'Why didn't she simply say when a man and a woman have sex?'

'Aur nahi toh kya?' Sushil said.

All we wanted to listen to were those few titillating words, but it was only the non-sexy stuff that we were hearing. Not that we had never heard them ever, but the pleasure of hearing it from our own teacher's mouth was incomparable to anything else. Till half an hour earlier, we had imagined that she would explain how to have sex to us; that she would talk about the reproductive organs—the ones she possessed and the ones we possessed. In a nutshell, we wanted to experience spoken porn, and hell!—she was treading nowhere close to it.

'. . . and that's how the baby is conceived inside a female.' She ended her lecture with that sensational line.

'Wow, the female got pregnant and there wasn't any mention of S–E–X. What was she producing—test-tube babies?' I whispered to Sushil in deep frustration.

People behind me overheard me and laughed.

Ten more minutes were left for the bell to ring. This was

usually the time for the question-and-answer session. Counting in the sensitivity of the topic and the presence of students like Sushil, Bio Ma'am decided it would be wise not to ask the class any question. So she let the entire class review the chapter on their own.

Some of us looked at Sushil, pushing him to utilize the remaining time and ask one more question. He refused.

A few chits and pieces of chalk were hurled at him. He managed to save himself from a few, but not all. He looked back, grinned and said, 'Bhak saala, main nahi puchhunga.'

'Last try, Sushil! Make her say something dirty,' someone in the crowd asked.

'Yes! Yes! You can do it!' everyone else cheered him on too, keeping their voices low. We treated him like he was our rock star.

All that flattery worked. Sushil agreed to give it a final try.

'Ma'am, one doubt!' Sushil said and raised his hand.

The boys looked at Sushil with great expectation. The girls wanted to run out of the class or hide themselves somewhere inside their bags. They looked really embarrassed. Bio Ma'am looked at her watch. She must have desperately wanted the bell to ring right then. But God was on our side.

'Yes?' She cleared her throat half-heartedly and agreed to listen to the question.

'Ma'am, I am not clear on how the male sperm lands up in the female's body,' he asked her with an innocent look, as if he seriously didn't know anything about it.

The entire class made a muffled 'Hooo!' sound in unison.

Now that was a checkmate. There was no way for Bio Ma'am to escape. She *had* to utter that word—'sex'— which we had been wanting her to say since the beginning of the class.

The excitement in the class had at once reached the extreme. By now, the girls had come to terms with the fact that they didn't have a choice but to adjust to the animal instincts of the boys. But Sushil's direct question was still difficult to digest for them. A few of the backbenchers first thought about clapping on Sushil's bravery, but changed their mind so that they could focus on what Ma'am was about to say.

Bio Ma'am looked uncomfortable and irritated with the question. She felt offended, but had no choice. She stood up angrily and asked the rest of the class, 'Anyone else has any other question?'

There was a silence. No one dared to ask anything.

'All right, then, I will answer Sushil's question,' she said, crossing her arms against her chest and walking into the aisle between the girls' row and the boys' row.

Sushil's eyes were twinkling and focused on her.

Bio Ma'am spoke, 'That happens when the male reproductive organ enters into the female reproductive organ.'

Now, that was the best line so far in the entire period! None of us said anything. But we enjoyed what we'd heard, hoping there would be more coming our way.

The teacher's eyes were fixed on Sushil. She waited for

him to tell her if his doubt had been cleared. But Sushil didn't say anything, so she continued to talk: 'And this physical act between a male and a female is known as having sex! That's what you wanted to hear?'

That was an 'Aaahhhh' moment for us. Three-fourth of the class would have achieved orgasm right at that sentence.

Bio Ma'am paused for a while and then resumed, 'We all came from our parents in that way. And that's how you too were born, Sushil. And, years from now, that's how our next generation will take birth. And, years from now, that's how your children will be born.'

She kept waiting for Sushil to acknowledge her answer, but Sushil, all of a sudden, had gone blank. He didn't expect that sort of answer to come from a teacher. I think he was not even sure if Ma'am was through with her answer, or if there was anything else to be added. Exactly after ten seconds of peace, when Sushil was sure that Ma'am didn't have anything further to say, he came up with a confused and funny response: 'Oh, okay, okay!'

And he sat down. Our fun for that class had come to an end.

The bell rang. A unanimous moan of 'Oh, nooo!' went around the class. Bio Ma'am wrapped up her handbag, books and attendance register as the rest of us stared at her.

'Complete the homework mentioned at the end of the chapter, and in the next class we will go through Chapter 11,' she said before leaving.

We quickly turned the pages of the textbook to see what was in Chapter 11.

Sushil looked back and whispered, 'The next chapter is on Sexually Transmitted Diseases!' He chuckled. 'Condoms bhi hai us mein . . . page eighty-nine, line number seven.'

And the rest of us geared up for yet another round of wild expectations and fun.

It is the eve of Janmashtami. It is close to midnight and I, along with my friends, am at the Krishna Mandir in Burla.

There are a lot of devotees around us. They all sit cross-legged on the floor of the sanctum of the temple. My friends and I, along with the other children, have occupied the last few rows. We are primarily in this temple to eat the delicious kheer and the temple prasad. It is a different kind of fun to meet your friends in the middle of the night at a place far away from home.

The sound of hymns and the peals of the temple bell resonate in my ears. The noise of the crowd adds to the din. But nothing beats the clamour in our side of the row. We are busy cracking jokes and teasing each other in the middle of the prayers. Time and again Panditji has been requesting us, on his mic, to be silent. Every time he says so, we drop into a temporary silence, and then soon return to our not-able-to-keep-quiet instincts.

The fourth time Panditji doesn't request us—he furiously commands all the children to come up to the front row. Every head turns to see us as we march in. We feel humiliated. If it was not for the kheer, we would have all left for our homes. We form a queue and, one by one, walk to the front row and occupy the part of the floor right in front of Panditji.

Sitting in the front row, we have no choice but to listen to the ancient katha that Panditji is narrating. It goes back to the Dvaapar Yuga.

Panditji is narrating the story of Lord Krishna's birth. He is telling us how, immediately after Devaki's marriage with Vasudeva, Devaki's brother Kansa listens to the Aakashvani—a heavenly prophecy uttered from somewhere behind the thundering sky— predicting the death of Kansa at the hands of Devaki and Vasudeva's eighth child. Terribly afraid, Kansa therefore sends the newly-wed couple behind bars.

The katha progresses. After describing Kansa's cruel and horrifying acts of murdering Devaki's first six children, Panditji has finally reached the event of Krishna's birth and all that happened on that auspicious night. He ends the katha with the following words: 'That is how, despite Kansa's efforts, Lord Krishna did arrive in this world. Bolo Bhagwaan Krishna ki—'

And everyone follows it with a loud '—jai!'

It is right at this time that my friends and I realize something and start laughing about it. All of a sudden, Panditji is again made aware of our presence. Annoyed, he asks us what we are up to.

One of us speaks up and tells Panditji that we have a doubt regarding the katha he has just narrated. Panditji is impressed with the attention we have paid to his storytelling. He announces that no one has ever expressed a problem in understanding any of his kathas, but, because we are children, he would love to address our doubt.

And then, in our group, there is a round of hurried whispers: 'Tu puchh na! Nahi, nahi, tu puchh!'

Panditji points his finger at me, selecting me to put forth our unanimous doubt. I confer with my friends if I should really ask what we have come up with. They all nod a yes.

'Panditji, after hearing the prophecy, why did Kansa lock up Devaki and Vasudeva in a prison?' I ask.

'Very good question, beta! You mean you are wondering why Kansa simply didn't kill the two of them and avoid further risks to his life?' Panditji goes on a different tangent altogether and continues to answer his own question. '. . . See, beta, he loved his sister, Devaki, so he could not kill her; and neither could he turn her into a widow by killing Vasudeva. But then, he feared the arrival of Devaki and Vasudeva's child into this world. That's why he put them both in a prison, so that, as soon as their children arrived in this world, he could kill them one by one.'

'No, no, Panditji, you didn't get it. Actually, what we want to know is this—if Kansa feared the birth of Devaki and Vasudeva's child, why did he lock the two of them up in the same *prison at all? You know what I mean—the two of them—in the same prison?'*

As I clarify my question, I don't notice that the mic is right next to me, and that it is turned on! My voice has just managed to travel through the wires of that mic to the sound boxes installed inside the temple and the loudspeaker on the roof of the temple, from where it has been broadcasted across a radius of two kilometres!

Hundreds of people at the back break into laughter. Many more start whispering about our shamelessness—mine in particular.

Panditji stands there with a blank face. He has absolutely no idea of where we have landed him. We don't expect him to answer our question. But we want him to realize that it wasn't a good idea for him to have taken us on and moved us to the front row.

Right then, someone in our group shouts: 'Kheer milni shuru ho gayi hai . . . chalo, chalo!'

And we rush out to have our share.

11

Show and Tell

One afternoon, during the recess hours, when I returned to the classroom to have a drink of water, I saw a group of boys gathered at the back of the class. Four of them were from my class, two were seniors and one was a junior who was well known in the school for all the wrong reasons. Together they were standing in a circle and looking at something. Curious to know what they were doing, I walked towards them.

As soon as they heard my footsteps, they looked at me and then at each other. Then they suddenly started to hide what they had all been looking at. I noticed them shuffling the pages of what appeared to be a magazine to me. There was loud and hurried whispering, which died down by the time I reached them. Now there was complete silence. This looked unusual.

Manoj and Sushil looked at me. The latter's presence assured me that something suspicious was definitely going on there. I didn't wait for long and addressed my question to Sushil: 'Kya dekh raha hai tu?' [What are you looking at?] With a smile on my lips, I waited for an interesting answer.

'Abey kuch nahi, Sardaar. Aise hi timepass kar rahe hain,' [Nothing much, buddy. We were just biding our time] he tried to dismiss my doubt.

But as I kept walking towards them, their body language became uncomfortable.

'Sushil was narrating a non-veg joke. That's all,' said someone else from the group.

'Really? Share it with me also, then,' I chuckled.

By then I had reached quite close to them. I caught Manoj hiding something under the desk.

'What are you hiding?'

'Leave!' shouted Devinder, who was our senior. He gave me an angry look.

But I wasn't going to back off. 'This is my classroom. Why should I leave?' I shot back.

Incensed by my counter-argument, Devinder made his way towards me. He stared right into my eyes. I didn't move away, and stared right back. This could result in a serious scuffle.

But Sushil intervened.

'Don't! He is a good friend,' he said, stopping Devinder.

When everyone had cooled down, Sushil asked Manoj to 'take that thing out'.

Manoj gave him a doubtful look. He raised his eyebrows and stared at the faces of the others. Sushil nodded.

Finally, Manoj slipped his hands out from underneath the desk. When I saw what he was holding, I could not believe my eyes. That moment of my life was officially tagged as My Introduction to the World of Dirty Magazines.

It was a Hindi magazine. The name on the cover read *Manohar Raatein*.

Just below the title, there was a photo of a woman lying on her belly on a cosy-looking bed. She wore barely anything. Her bare back was arched and ended in curves which were the centre of attraction in the photo. A translucent, black-colored stole ran between her lower back and her toned thighs—and that was the only piece of clothing on her. She had perched her chin on her right hand, with the little finger gently held inside her mouth. She was looking right into the camera with a mysterious smile.

'Oh my God!' I exclaimed, as my mouth fell open. I stared at it, amazed, for more than a minute.

Sushil looked at my expression and smiled. It didn't bother me. After some more time, Sushil put his hand on my shoulder.

'Kya ho gaya be?' [What happened to you?] he laughed. The others joined him. The collective laughter distracted me from my reverie on those curves on the cover. And, soon, I remembered that I was in the classroom! I looked at the entrance and swallowed the lump that had formed in my throat.

'Don't worry; no one will get to know. Enjoy!' Sushil said. He still had his hand over my shoulder.

The little shyness in me had, by then, vanished. I adjusted my position in the circle to a place from where I could take a better look at the magazine.

Damn! She was sexy.

'Should I flip the page now?' asked Manoj, who was our man on the task.

Half of us answered yes, the other half said no. He waited for everyone to say yes, and, in the meantime, went ahead to mischievously run his fingers over that nude back in the picture.

Watching him do so, I felt disgusted. But a little later, for some reason, my disgust subsided. After a short while, I too wanted to run my fingers over that bare back.

'Turn the page, now!' shouted someone.

No one objected this time, and so Manoj turned the page.

'Kaun laaya hai ye?' I wanted to find out who had brought the magazine, when my eyes fell on the picture on the next page.

A South Indian girl in a tight black blouse yanked us up to the next level of excitement.

Everyone sighed: 'Aaaaah!'

The woman's small blouse had tiny sleeves and a deep

neckline. There were hooks running down the front of the blouse, but only the two lowest hooks had been fastened. The upper part of the blouse had been left unhooked, revealing what the woman was wearing inside. The voluptuousness of her figure was revolting against the constricting piece of cloth. It was as if her body was trying to break away and set itself free. Below her waistline, with her left hand, she had hitched up her skirt over her thighs.

'Sushil laaya hai,' Manoj replied, as he tried to pull the magazine closer to him in order to take a better look.

'Every page you turn now, she is going to throw away one piece of cloth.'

I don't know who said that. But that statement put us into so much excitement that we were quickly out of patience and started snatching at the magazine among ourselves.

'Why are you pulling?' all of us shouted at each other; but not a single one of us was willing to let go! The picture of one naked girl had brought out our animal instincts.

'Abey, idhar kar!'

'Give it to me!'

'Oh, come on!'

'Abey, phatt jayegi magazine!' [Hey, the magazine will tear!]

We'd got ourselves into a chaotic, screaming mess.

Soon, Devinder flung into action. He took advantage of his seniority and brought the situation under control. First, he shouted everyone down. Then, he suggested circulating the magazine among us in the round-robin fashion, so that everyone got a fair chance to look at the pictures.

We all agreed to the suggestion. But, the very next moment, we got into a quarrel over who should be the first one to avail of that opportunity.

Devinder had an answer to that as well. He chose himself for this privilege. The rest of us unhappily allowed him to go ahead.

'Now you are only seeing the pictures, but read the stories from this magazine also! Mast hai!' [They're fantastic!] Sushil advised me, as I awaited my turn.

'Really?'

'After reading them, you will have to head straight to the bathroom,' he chuckled.

Unable to understand what he meant, I asked, 'Why would I need to go to the bathroom?'

A few of the other guys broke into laughter.

'Abey, baccha hai ye abhi!' [Hey, he's still a kid!] someone said. Devinder was laughing too, as he handed over the magazine to the person next in queue.

I wanted to remind him of his age, and, more importantly, the fact that he was still in school, because he had failed several classes.

'Haven't you done it, ever?' Sushil asked me inquisitively.

By then, the magazine had arrived in my hands. I didn't care what Sushil's question meant. I was just excited that it was finally my turn to look at the magazine. But, before I could go through the picture carefully and closely, the peon outside the principal's office started ringing the bell. I cursed him in my head.

I was worried that people would walk in any time, and that killed my excitement. I didn't want to rush through the magazine. I didn't want to ruin the pleasure of watching a dark-complexioned girl of about twenty-five years slowly taking off her clothes with every turn of the page. I wanted to savour it, slowly. So I closed it and half-heartedly handed it back to Sushil.

For the rest of the day that naked girl danced in my head. When the Maths Sir drew a triangle, I drew a triangle as well; and, along with it, I also drew the sketch of that girl in the corner of the page. When he was teaching how to apply the rules of trigonometry in order to find out the length of the shadow of the tree, when the height of the tree and the angle of sunrays was given, I was busy colouring her blouse and skirt.

I elbowed Sushil, who sat next to me, to show him my creativity. He was busy taking notes. So I elbowed him again. He looked at me.

The painter in me looked at him, and, with great pride, pointed out to him my freshly drawn Mona Lisa. He looked at her and smiled. He spent some time examining my artwork, and then did a little touch-up himself. He made the cleavage a bit deeper, looked back at me and winked.

'Perfect!' I whispered, admiring his talent and superior knowledge of the subject. The next moment, the two of us broke into quiet laughter.

At 4 p.m., when school ended, I approached Sushil to have a private conversation. I wanted to borrow his magazine. I thought I was smart to think of going through it in the privacy of my home.

It turned out that I was the last one in the group to have that conversation with Sushil. He had already promised to lend his magazine to everyone for the next few days. He gave me a date which was eight days later.

I had never ever waited that desperately for anything else. *Never, ever!*

~

That evening, after I came back from school, I lied to my mother that I was not feeling well. It was my excuse for not going to the tuition classes.

Mom gripped my hand in her palms and then touched my forehead. She wanted to verify if I had fever. There wasn't any.

'It's a bad headache, Mom. I might be coming down with something,' I said.

'Have a Disprin after you finish your bread and butter, and then take rest,' she advised me concernedly, and put a tablet on my plate along with half a glass of water.

Every evening, my parents would go to the gurdwara to offer their evening prayers. That's when a lot of other people also came to the gurdwara. It usually took them an hour before they got back. In a while, my brother too left for his tuition classes.

I flushed the Disprin down the kitchen washbasin, locked the main door of our house and headed straight for my bed. I piled up two pillows under my head, after which I grabbed my schoolbag, which was lying in the other corner of the bed.

It was time for me to enjoy *Manohar Raatein*.

My happy hour had just begun. I was euphoric about this private entertainment I had planned for myself. It didn't take me long to submerge myself in the world of pleasure. I returned to the page where that dark-complexioned girl had made her seductive entry.

I zoomed in to take a closer look at her poised body, her tight blouse and her hitched-up skirt. I observed the body parts that were visible. I imagined the ones that were not.

For some reason, I was in love with her blouse, maybe because it had little to hide and a lot to reveal. On the top of all this, her naughty smile was driving me crazy. I flipped through the pages with great expectation. I knew what to expect next, yet I wanted to be surprised.

On the next page she had moved into a bathroom. There was a mirror behind her showing off her shapely back. I was already seeing her front. The washbasin behind her had a lot of toiletries. A bathtub, on her right, perfectly filled in the scene.

This time, those last two hooks had also fallen open. The blouse hung limply on her body. A pair of black lacy straps ran down her shoulders, revealing a lot of net in front, in between the folds of her open blouse.

My body had started reacting to those visuals. I felt different. I felt as if I wanted to disconnect from the rest of the world and enjoy what I was busy doing. I didn't want to be bothered about anything else in that moment. I just focused on that girl.

I moved my fingers over her picture and circled her belly button. I wanted to feel her in person. The mere imagination was so much fun.

She still hitched her skirt up with her hand, but the posture of her legs had changed this time. Her legs were crossed and her body had tilted sideways. The skirt had slipped further down. A black elastic band peeked from above her waist. It was too sexy to be missed.

Each time the camera had aimed at the girl, she had looked straight into it. Her eyes revealed confidence—a notorious one! I imagined that I wasn't only imagining. And that she was actually looking at me. That she was smiling, knowing what was happening to me. I was getting hard and this different kind of feeling was just irresistible. I turned the page.

Those black straps had now slipped off her shoulders and were down to her elbows. She had allowed that to happen. The blouse was already on the floor. For the very first time in my life I was looking at a topless woman. It didn't matter if she was only in the photograph.

I rolled around in my bed to change my position. I lay on my stomach, rested my chin on the pillow and held the magazine in front of my eyes. I pulled the blanket from the edge of the bed, rolled it up and sandwiched it in between my legs. It was an exceedingly sensual moment for me to observe her vital parts left unclothed. I spent a lot of time just observing the skin and the shape.

The next half an hour was full of a few more sensual visuals that aroused erotic feelings within me. As I progressed, I felt as if she was hypnotizing me. I enjoyed her company on every page.

By the last page, she had run out of all her clothes. To me, she looked her best then. Her young, poised body was partly submerged in bathtub water. Her right leg loosely hung outside the tub, and a tiny stream of water dripped down her leg on to the floor.

I was looking at a fully naked woman, in the most erotic posture, offering me the best possible view of the most important parts of her body.

But then, something strange happened with me. Those erotic feelings had turned into some sort of a black hole and were trying to suck me into them! It was difficult to understand what I was feeling at that moment. I found myself in the extremes of pleasure, from where it was hard to come back. I felt as if a lot of anxiety had concentrated somewhere in me, and that I would explode because of it! I was badly in need of giving vent to what I had contained within me. I felt uncomfortable. I wanted to calm down.

I knew boys got hard when they experienced erotic feelings. I too had experienced such feelings quite a few times before. But, that day, it was strangely different. I wanted to help myself but didn't know how to deal with the situation. In some sort of nervousness, I slipped my hand into my shorts. It seemed natural for me to do so.

Right then, I felt I was going to pee. I tried to control it and run to the bathroom. But my body didn't allow me any time! Before I could even get up from my bed, I felt my body had flushed out something. I pulled out my hand. It wasn't wet. It was sticky. I could not understand what that was.

A sense of horror took over me.

What has happened to me? Worried, I had started talking to myself.

I unzipped my shorts to see what had happened to me. I had absolutely no idea of what that semi-liquid substance that had spilled into my clothes might be.

'Oh God!'

Unable to make any sense of it, a flood of thoughts crossed my mind. I believed it was a bad disease. I believed that God had punished me for reading that dreadful magazine. I knew I was in deep trouble.

I panicked.

I ran to the bathroom and cleaned myself. All this while, my heart was begging for forgiveness from God. 'I won't read it again. Please! Please, God!'

It was a silent, one-sided conversation. I wondered if I should tell Mom about this. But then I wondered how I would explain it to her.

Right then there was a knock on the door.

I was terrified beyond measure now. I had to be quick! But quick with what—was the question. I looked at myself in the mirror. My hands shivered as I tried to clean my shorts. In my state of panic, I could not clean it properly and threw it in the lot of laundry clothes. I came out of the bathroom and ran to open the door. At the last moment, I noticed the magazine on the bed. I changed course and ran again to hide it inside my bag.

There was another knock on the door.

'Oh God!'

By the time I opened the door, I was breathless.

'Why did you shut the door?'

It was my mother.

'Oh . . . ummm . . . hmm . . . just like that.'

'Aa, le, parshaad le le.' She offered me the prasad, the offerings from the gurdwara.

Because of what I was involved in till a few minutes ago,

taking the prasad with my hands didn't seem like a nice idea to me. So I refused.

'I will have it a little later.'

'Tera sir theek ho gaya?' she asked about my headache, on her way to the TV room.

'Not yet,' I told her, and went back to my bed.

I covered myself with the blanket. All this while, I was worried about my health. I had decided to secretly consult a doctor the next day. To overcome my embarrassment of describing the situation to the doctor, I thought of taking Sushil along with me. After all, it was his magazine that had cast a curse over me.

I didn't have a comfortable sleep that night. I was deeply disturbed—firstly because of the experience itself, but, secondly, because I could not share it with anyone in my family. I did not even dare to urinate before I went to sleep that night! I was afraid that I would again pass the mysterious fluid that I had a few hours back. Time and again, I would wake up with a start and recall the fearful event of the evening.

Fortunately enough, till the time the sun came up, I didn't experience anything more unusual. My morning stint in the bathroom also went fine. After holding it in for a good twelve hours, I had finally peed—and a lot of it! By the time I reached school, I felt I was out of danger. And interestingly, after having a chat with Sushil, I came to know that I didn't need him to take me to a doctor. Sushil himself turned out to be my much-needed doctor!

That day, I realized that you don't always learn the important lessons of life in the company of decent friends. Some key lessons of life are learnt in the company of notorious friends like Sushil.

Sushil started with making me comfortable. His statement that 'I too had experienced the same' calmed me down. He explained to me that what I had experienced was one of the signs of a boy reaching puberty. I also learnt that girls of our age experienced a similar shock when they witnessed the blood during their first menstrual cycle. I had been quite unaware of all these scary signs of puberty. After half an hour's chat, I was happy to find out that I was normal. Moreover, I became confident that I had stepped into adulthood. Slowly, a hesitant pride made its way within me.

Sushil surprised me with his wisdom on this subject. Apart from his 'gyaan' he had another surprise for me. He gave it to me after the last class of the day.

It was another magazine.

12

First Crush

It was the middle of the afternoon and the class was in a happy mood. The third period had just got over and we knew that English Sir, who was supposed to take the next period, was absent that day. As soon as the bell rang, Amit, who was the monitor in charge of the class, flung into action and ran towards the staff room.

We wanted him to ensure that the English period was declared as the Games period. Given the fact that the fourth period was followed by a forty-minute recess, it would have been a prolonged period of fun for all of us.

Transforming an educational period into a recreational period is an art. It doesn't just happen. It needs a context setting, followed by a problem statement, followed by probable solutions, followed by creating an opportunity wherein the most desired solution for students fits in well with the teacher as well. Of course, it is a step-by-step process.

But Amit was technically challenged in understanding and implementing this vital process. That duffer ended up asking our class teacher in a room full of other teachers, 'Ma'am, shall we go for Games—as English Sir is absent? Yesterday, when History Sir was absent, we had gone for Games!'

The class teacher denied permission right away and appointed another teacher to attend to our class. Gurpreet, who was the girls' monitor for the class and had accompanied Amit to the staff room, updated us on Amit's stupidity.

'Why did you tell her that we got a Games period only yesterday, when History Sir was absent?' someone from the back shouted at our monitor.

Someone else hurled another accusation at Amit, and that successfully set up a chain reaction of allegations. One by one, everyone in the class joined in on yelling at Amit. In schools, students always seem to gang up against one. We had mastered the art of beating up a dead horse.

'When will this month end—so that we can get a change from this dumb monitor!' someone from the girls' end shouted.

'On the thirtieth!' someone else responded. Everybody laughed.

There was utter chaos in the classroom, which lasted for

the next ten minutes. Then, all of a sudden, there was silence. It was because of the arrival of a teacher who we knew taught English in the primary section of our school.

I had always found her to be very attractive and had secretly followed her a couple of times around the school campus. I used to stop and admire her whenever she would pass me by. She wasn't the most beautiful teacher in the school; I knew that Bio Ma'am was considered far more beautiful than her. But, for me, there was something about her that attracted me to her more than to Bio Ma'am. I never figured out what that attraction was. I didn't even know her name.

It was a beautiful feeling to see her step into our class. Her presence brought a smile to my lips and left my eyes twinkling with pleasure. I now wanted to hug Amit for his idiocy.

She was tall and her sari made her look graceful. However, not everyone was as excited to see her.

'Good afternoon, Ma'am!' the students greeted her half-heartedly.

She replied with a wholehearted 'Gooood afternooooooooon, students!' carried over from her way of teaching the primary classes.

That was the first time I heard her voice. I loved that as well!

She took her seat and the class settled in. My eyes were glued to her. It was my opportunity to watch her for a long time—something I never got to do earlier. She had wheatish skin. Her hair was tied into a ponytail that ran down her back just like a horse's tail. She was slim, which was another reason why she looked so tall. She was taller than me; I guess by a foot. She didn't wear a lot of accessories—just a wristwatch and a sleek chain around her neck. In all aspects, she was simple yet elegant, and a little more attractive than average.

'I will be taking today's class on behalf of your English Sir!' she announced.

In my heart, I wished for Sir to be absent for the rest of the week!

She asked us to open our books. Then she got up from her chair, readjusted her sari and tucked the end of it into her waist. That gave me a glimpse of her slender waist.

How I wanted to move to the first bench now!

She held the book nicely in one hand and played with the piece of chalk with her other hand. Her soft voice was a treat to my ears. She slipped into the gap in front of the blackboard. I followed her movements as well as her words.

She started teaching nouns. After setting up the context, she went on to explain the same on the board. She wrote down the heading 'Noun', and drew several branches from it, in order to explain the various types of nouns.

Just then, the power went off. *Damn!* Everyone sighed. Firstly, they had not been able to play, and now this! However, power cuts were usual in the area of our school.

The moment the summer temperatures soared, this started happening. The rotating fans in the classroom came to rest and so did their noise.

Ma'am continued to write on the board and the lesson continued. While the rest of the class was watching the decelerating fans in dismay, my eyes were stuck on her. I was busy fulfilling my desire to look at her body—every bit of it. I enjoyed observing her body language—every move of hers. She had an amazing back. Time and again, as she moved towards the blackboard, her hair bounced on her back, seductively hiding one part of her back while revealing another. I wanted to smell the hair that played this game of hide-and-seek with her back. I liked the way she turned towards us each time after writing down another form of the noun on the board. I enjoyed the way she tossed the piece of chalk and played with it in her hand. Every time she did that, her wristwatch slipped up and down her arm.

My brain didn't register anything she taught. I simply copied down what she wrote on the blackboard in my notebook. There were various forms of the noun, not a single one of which registered in my mind.

One moment, she accelerated my heartbeat when she walked down the aisle where I sat. I felt I wasn't prepared for this moment! One half of my mind didn't want to lose the opportunity to look at her from up close, and the other half felt too shy to do so.

A thousand butterflies flitted around inside my stomach,

the moment she stopped right beside me. *Oh boy!*—I was able to smell her now. The perfume she was wearing struck down the shy half of my mind, which was too embarrassed to look at her. So I stared at her. I breathed in that fragrance, imagining how those vapours would have originated from her body and touched her smooth skin. The butterflies in my stomach now seductively flapped their tiny wings. I guess they wanted to break free. I turned my head to gaze fully at her.

From that side, I saw her flat stomach behind the drape of her sari, something that wasn't visible from the front. My eyes joyfully scanned her waist. Her skin looked soft. Tiny sweat drops were forming under the border of her blouse and slipping down to her waist. I wanted to touch her— right there. I wanted to closely smell that sweat infused with the fragrance of her body.

At one instance, when she had changed the support of her body from one leg to another, I secretly noticed her belly button, an inch above where she had tucked in her sari. There was no point in peeling my eyes away. I wanted to put my finger in her belly button and feel the moisture in it. There was so much for me to savour in the moment. Her presence next to me was taking away my breath. She had hypnotized me, without any intention to do so. My body was just physically present in the class. My mind was quite obviously elsewhere. It was busy imagining all sorts of thrills. I couldn't listen to anything either. I saw whatever I imagined. My sense organs had gone on an overload. They only came back to the real world when Sushil, who still sat next to me, pulled at my arm.

'Abey, answer her?'

'Huh! What!' I was, all of a sudden, brought back to reality.

I looked back at Sushil and raised my eyebrows, wondering what had happened.

The class laughed. I failed to understand why. I thought of joining in with their laugh, but soon I guessed that maybe *I* was the subject of their laughter.

'She asked you a question?' Sushil said politely, and continued to smile.

I looked ahead of me. The teacher was looking right into my eyes! And it was not the look I was longing for! A mocking smile played at the corner of her lips.

A thought crossed my mind—had she found out what was going on in my mind? Had she come to know of my thoughts . . . about her? It was a scary thought. Scared and embarrassed, I looked around.

The mass laughter came to a stop.

'Will you answer the question?' the lady, whose belly button I wanted to touch, asked me again.

'Bb . . . bb . . . yes, Ma'am,' I blabbered and stood up with a completely blank mind and sweaty palms.

Everyone waited, probably wondering what I was about to say.

I had never wanted this to happen; not with the only teacher who was so special to me. How could I stand being humiliated in front of her, and, more importantly, by her?

I looked at Sushil and gestured with my chin, asking him to reveal the question. He whispered something that didn't make any sense to me.

So I gathered my guts and managed to ask the teacher, 'Aaa . . . Ma'am, what was the question?'

Another round of laughter followed my question. Ma'am too started laughing—her tinkling laughter revealing her pearly white teeth. I, too, smiled in response.

She didn't answer my question. Instead, she asked, 'What's your name?'

'Ma'am, Ravinder Singh.' I adjusted the knot of my tie with style as I introduced myself to my favourite teacher.

'So, Ravinder, where was your mind while I was teaching?' She killed the smile halfway on my face.

How could I tell her where my mind was—and who was in my mind, and what all I had been thinking about her?

'Aa . . . no . . . no . . . nothing . . . aa . . . nothing as such, Ma'am!' I had nothing to say and everything to hide.

She kept looking at me. I fixed my gaze on my table, embarrassed. A few of my classmates kept smiling at my condition.

'Sit down!' she said.

'Ma'am?' I wanted to verify if she really meant that.

'I said, "Sit down," Ravinder, and be attentive in class!' she advised sternly.

'Yes, Ma'am.'

I sat down immediately, and then stood up the next moment to say, 'Sorry, Ma'am,' and sat down again. The class again broke into a final round of laughter.

Ma'am proceeded with the explanation of a few more forms of the noun. I looked at Sushil. He grabbed this opportunity to make fun of me.

'Beta, sab pata hai mujhe tera dhyaan kahaan tha!' [I know exactly where your attention was!] he said, smugly.

'What do you mean?' I asked.

'Abey, ghoor ghoor ke dekh raha tha Ma'am ko.' He had noticed me staring at the teacher.

'Aisa kuch nahi hai,' I rejected his insinuation and turned my eyes to the book.

'Oh really!' he mocked me.

I didn't answer.

'So it means you don't like her?'

'Chup kar ja bhai, padh lene de,' I asked him to not disturb me and let me study. I had to play it safe. I ignored any further conversation with him.

In a little while, the teacher rubbed off the entire blackboard and went ahead to write down examples of each form of the noun. I heard a murmur behind me. Ideally, I would have wanted to be a part of it, but after whatever had happened, I didn't want to indulge in anything that she wouldn't like. So I didn't pay heed to the talks in the back bench. I concentrated on taking notes of the examples. I wanted to redeem myself in Ma'am's eyes. I decided not to let go of any opportunity to answer any of her questions; or, if not that, then to ask an intelligent one myself. Maybe that would undo the negative impression she had formed of me in her mind, I thought.

I could feel the whispers behind my back move from one bench to the other. As yet they were limited to the boys' side of the class. I looked back and saw a few anxious faces. I wondered what they were up to.

I was busy taking notes, when Sushil interrupted me by asking if I was not having fun. 'Abey, tu mazey nahi le raha?'

'What?'

'Look at her now,' he said, and pointed with his chin towards the teacher, who was still writing on the board.

At first, I failed to understand what Sushil was pointing at, but it didn't take me long to realize.

It had been long since the fans had been turned off and the heat of the summer afternoon had further raised the room temperature. The sweat on Ma'am's body had made her white blouse translucent, revealing the bra that she wore inside. And that was the subject of discussion among the boys of the class.

I felt terrible. I looked around myself and found everyone staring at her back. Somehow this didn't feel right. I felt uncomfortable. It made me let go of my attention on what she had been teaching. I wanted to stop them all from taking her in like that.

I felt as if there was an undefined relationship between her and me; and that I should do something to protect her from all this. But I couldn't think of doing anything. I only prayed for the power supply to return soon; and if not that, then for the bell to ring soon; and if not that, then for Ma'am to turn towards us and hold the same position for the rest of the class.

'Look at that sexy pink thing inside her blouse!' Sushil whispered, with obvious lust.

'Shut up!' I whispered angrily, as I couldn't hold back my temper.

The smile on his face evaporated as soon as he saw that I was serious about what I had said. I guess he hadn't expected that reaction from me.

'Don't say anything like that about her,' I warned him.

He gave me a blank look and then turned around to update our common friends: 'Sardaar paagal ho gaya hai!' [This guy has gone mad] and narrated my reaction to them.

The teacher caught our side-conversations, turned back and asked, 'Any problem there?'

No one said anything. She waited, and then resumed writing on the board. My friends behind my bench joined Sushil in laughing at me. They became wilder and started talking cheaply about her.

For a while, I didn't react, knowing that they were doing this only to tease me. But that didn't stop them from having fun. I was getting terribly upset, listening to all that they were saying about her. I could not help myself from objecting to their filthy blabber.

Then Sushil crossed all limits when he said, 'I am going to imagine her tonight in my bed.' This was beyond my limit of tolerance. I jumped up to clutch his neck in my hands.

My anger stunned Sushil. He hadn't expected that from me. The moment he realized what had just happened, he held my wrist in his hand and tried to escape my grip. Someone from the bench behind us immediately jumped in to separate the two of us and stop the fight.

But I was out of control. Never, ever in my life earlier had I behaved this way!

'I asked you to stop,' I said, as I gripped his neck with one hand and punched him in the chest with the other.

Sushil didn't wait for too long to react. The last thing he said was, 'Mujhe maarega is ke liye tu!' [You will hit me for this!] before he hurled a blow which narrowly missed my head.

The teacher turned around when she heard the commotion. She saw me and Sushil exchange blows.

'Get up, you two!' she shouted sternly. She then placed her book on the table and walked towards us.

'Out! Out, the two of you!'

'Ma'am, he hit me first. You can ask anyone!' Sushil claimed with confidence.

In her anger, Ma'am immediately shifted her eyes to me. 'Did you hit him first?' she asked me pointedly.

I was silent, staring down at the desk.

'Tell me! Did you hit him first?' she repeated her question in anger.

'Yes, Ma'am,' I said and kept looking at my desk.

'Now tell me why you did that,' she crossed her arms against her chest and questioned me.

'Because he was talking dirty,' I answered softly.

'No, Ma'am, I didn't say anything!' Sushil intervened.

Ma'am signalled for Sushil to keep quiet and asked me, 'What did he say?'

I didn't say anything. *How could I?*

She asked me again, '*What did he say?*'

I still didn't utter a word.

She probably found my silence insulting, and, reluctant to discuss the issue any further, she commanded, 'Get out, Ravinder!' showing me the door.

I looked at her. Her hand was still pointing towards the door. I looked at Sushil and then the backbenchers.

'*Now!*' Ma'am reminded me.

Whispers filled the room.

I closed my notebook, put the cap on my pen and walked out of the class without any debate.

That was the very first time I had been punished in my new school. Ironically, I had been punished by the teacher I liked the most!

Leaning against the wall of the classroom and looking into the barren campus, I thought over how I had thought of impressing her when the class had begun, and what it all had turned into. I wondered why I felt so offended when Sushil talked badly about this Ma'am. He had been talking about someone whom I hardly knew. I had never been this violent and hit anyone for someone else. I was not sure if I would have hit my benchmate for any other teacher.

The bell rang and the period ended. The entire school broke for recess. The teacher walked out and looked at me.

'Go in,' she said. 'Don't do that, ever!'

She still seemed angry with me. I kept staring at her as she walked down the corridor and then took a left turn towards the staff room.

I realized that I had ruined it all. But I still believed what I did had been right. I would do it again if someone talked badly about her. I would bang his head the next time, I decided.

That period had changed a lot of things for me. A bunch of boys believed that I had fallen for that teacher. I denied it when they said so to my face, but inside I felt nice when people associated me with her.

The only good thing was that English Ma'am now knew my name. Out of the whole class, she would remember me. The sad thing was that she would remember me for all the wrong reasons. I was no more at the starting line of the race to impress her. Instead, I was on the opposite side of the starting line.

The biggest difference that the period brought in for me was that Sushil and I had broken up our friendship. It had all happened in a very short time frame. Just one period back, we had been really good friends. A period later, the two of us were talking to everybody but each other.

When I walked inside the class, I overheard Sushil telling our common friends how I had forgotten our friendship for a teacher. '. . . Ma'am ke chakkar mein apne dost pe haath uthaaya!'

I heard more.

'He is always so calm and jolly. I thought you hit him first,' someone in the group reacted to Sushil's comment.

'Yes, he isn't of that nature. It's still impossible for me to believe what he did!'

I packed my bag and walked out of the classroom with my tiffin box. That day I didn't eat my lunch—I fed it to a cow outside our school campus.

One morning, I am at school.

It is the fifth of the month, the last day for collecting the monthly school fee. But the school clerk, who does this job of collection, has been absent for a week because he's been ill.

Moments after the prayer assembly, the principal announces that all the class teachers, while taking the attendance, will collect the fees from the students in the first period. The receipts will be distributed to us later.

Apart from that clerk and the principal, no one in my new school knows that I don't pay for my education. It has been a well-kept secret so far. In the past, whenever my friends had asked me to go along with them to pay my fee, I had always made some excuse and slipped away. Usually, I would tell them that I had already paid my fee for that month. Now I am in a fix.

A little later, I am inside the classroom. I am worried about getting exposed in front of everyone. I feel cold.

What will they think of me? That I have been telling them lies for past so many months? That whatever they have to pay for, I enjoy it all for free?

Scores of thoughts are passing through my mind. One moment, I want to run out of the classroom and let the class teacher mark me absent. But, right then, she makes eye contact with me. So I sit back.

She starts calling the roll numbers, one by one.

My classmates walk down to her to deposit their fees, one by one.

Uncomfortably I sit, waiting for my turn, and wishing something could interrupt the process. All of a sudden, I think of something and slip my hand into my pocket. I bring out whatever money I'm carrying. I count it. It is seventeen rupees, in all. I nudge Sushil, who is busy talking to someone behind him. He asks me to wait for a while. I tell him it is urgent. He turns to me and asks what has happened.

I ask him for some money that I can borrow.

He checks his pockets and tells me that he has some twenty bucks. He hands me two ten-rupee notes. That brings my total up to thirty-seven rupees. I am still short by a lot of money.

I reach out to Amit. I know he is the richest boy in our class. Unfortunately, he can't help. He says he had cleared his canteen balance this morning, and has only kept enough for his fee. Looking at my disappointed face, he promises to lend me any amount I ask for, but only the next day.

But tomorrow will be too late. In fact, tomorrow I won't even need his money. I need it right at this moment, so that I can pay the fee and save myself from the embarrassment. I am thinking fast, but time is racing faster than me.

And then, the moment arrives. The class teacher calls out my roll number.

I have no idea what to say. I hand over those twenty rupees back to Sushil and pull out an old piece of paper from the first pocket of my bag. I fold it in my palm and start walking towards the class teacher.

I take my time to reach her desk. I don't know what to tell her. I am thinking hard, but the panic in my heart isn't letting me think. When I reach the desk, I see a lot of money on the table. The class teacher waits for me to hand over my share.

With a blank face, I lean towards her. I almost whisper my words. She doesn't hear me clearly, so she asks me to say it again. Avoiding to look at the rest of the class, I quietly repeat what I had said earlier.

'What do you mean you don't pay your fees?' she asks back, loud and clear. She is confused and wants me to explain what I just said.

Shit!!!

The people in the first few benches have heard the question. They are surprised and start discussing it among themselves. In no time, the news travels to the other end of the class. All ears and eyes are on me now.

I am not able to make eye contact with anyone in the class.

The class teacher calls my name again. My explanation is still due.

I tell her that I don't pay the fee to the school.

'But why?' she asks me, removing her spectacles from her eyes.

'We are poor. My father can't afford the fee,' I say, unfolding the piece of paper in my hand and putting it on her desk for her to see.

It is the application letter for the dismissal of my fee, approved by the principal and the school committee.

I do not raise my head. I avoid meeting anyone's eye. I don't have the guts to do it. The entire class breaks into a series of whispers. They know it all by now. I have alienated myself from everyone.

A little later, the class teacher asks me to go back to my seat. She hands the letter back to me.

I go back to my seat. I fold the letter back into its original folds and put it in my shirt's pocket. All this while, I am looking at the ground. I slip into my seat silently.

When the first period ends, I prepare myself for the difficult questions that are bound to come my way from my classmates.

I wait for the worst.

But, to my surprise, everyone interacts with me as if nothing has happened!

No one asks me anything about my fee. Never, ever!

13

One Dark Day

If I remember it well, it was around mid-April that year when I had my first chance to see a movie at a theatre. The afternoon was pleasant, and my friends and I had gone to watch the matinee show. It was a totally unplanned event. In fact, our final exams were going on and we had one on that day as well—history exam, the most boring of all.

As usual, by 12.30 p.m. most of the students had arrived at school. The exam was scheduled to start sharp at 1 p.m. The schoolbags on our shoulders that day were light, as we carried only the relevant study material for the exam. The question papers and clipboards in everyone's hands transmitted the anxiety of exams in the air. A last-minute sharpening of pencils or checking the ink in our pens kept most of us busy.

One could see the before-the-exam nervousness on practically everyone's face. A handful of confident top-rankers also tried to fake the nervousness. Most of them, as usual, kept saying, 'I don't know what will happen in today's exam. I don't remember anything that I studied last night.'

It was their modus operandi to make the others appear well prepared just before the exam, so that they didn't revise any more, while they themselves kept revising, saying they were nervous. It was a trick that everyone knew about, and yet it was practised.

On the other hand, the low-rank holders of the class were, as usual, also confident about their preparation. Most of them, as usual, kept saying, 'History is a story. We will write one for every question—big deal!'

Standing among that noisy herd, in front of the huge entrance area of the school, the rest of us were testing each other on the 'Dates and Events' section from the appendix of the book. That was the best last-minute brush-up one could do before a history exam.

Amit asked me one question. 'When was Mahatma Gandhi born?'

'Second October,' I replied, recalling the public holiday.

'Abey, year bataa! Date nahi.' He had asked for the year and not just the date.

'Year? Hmm . . . 1940,' I answered. Then, looking at the expression on his face, I quickly said, '. . . nahi, 1937.'

He chuckled and said, 'You mean Gandhiji was ten years old when we got our freedom!'

Overhearing that, Gurpreet, who was standing close to us, started laughing. However, she also didn't know the answer.

'1869,' Amit updated us.

That felt like an insult to me—humiliated in front of a third person, that too a girl.

'Okay, okay, now let me ask you one.' I opened my book and asked him to close his.

'Chal bataa, first Battle of Panipat kab hui thi?' I questioned him about the date of the historic battle.

'1526!' he answered instantaneously, with a victorious smile. I verified his answer. He was absolutely right. My ego was bruised—he knew more than me!

'And the second Battle of Panipat?' I quizzed him back, hoping he would be wrong this time.

'Hmm ... second ... battle ... 15—yes, 1556?' he blurted out the date as soon as his brain fished it out of the calendar installed in his memory.

Unfortunately, he was right again.

His level of confidence shattered mine. In my mind, there were only two ways to feel comfortable in the moments before the exam. First, if you could correctly answer the questions that someone asked you. And second, if you couldn't answer someone else's question, that someone else should not be able to answer yours as well.

For me, neither of the two had worked. So I raised the bar and looked for a difficult question. This was to restore my confidence, however small.

'Will you be comfortable answering anything from the Mughal period?'

Amit nodded.

'When did Anaarkali die?'

He broke into laughter immediately. 'We don't have Anaarkali in our books, must be Razia Sultana. Check it out!'

I took another look through the 'Dates and Events' page and, exactly three seconds later, I plunged into oceans of jealousy as well as sadness—he was right! *What a blunder!*

The bell rang and interrupted our Q&A session. We now had to go inside the examination room and take up our designated seats. I closed my book and looked at Amit. He asked me, 'Should I tell you the date when Razia Sultana died?'

That was too much to bear!

'No need. Leave it. All the best!' I said and ran inside. I heard Amit shouting 'All the best' to me behind my back. *Did it matter now?*

We were seated in our respective classrooms to take the exam. But then, all of a sudden, things changed—some Morarji Desai had passed away. And one of our teachers, who was the invigilator for my class, broadcast the news that the history exam had been postponed to the next day.

I didn't know who Morarji Desai was and what his death had to do with our history exam. My best guess was that he must have been on our school committee. There were a few more like me in the crowd, but some intelligent soul updated all of us that he was the fourth prime minister of India! I am sure, on hearing that, Amit would have added that date to the calendar in his memory!

Anyway, the conclusion was that now we had time on our hands. Mature human beings mourn someone's death. Immature ones like us go out for a movie.

And that's what we did!

Everyone realized that it was pointless to reread history. What difference would it make? And, anyhow, we had the whole night and the entire morning of the next day to revise the syllabus.

Laxmi Talkies was playing *Karan Arjun*. I had never watched a movie in a theatre till then. My hometown, Burla, didn't have any theatre—the only one in the town had shut down long back. I wondered if I had enough money to watch the show. Sushil told me that Laxmi Talkies was the cheapest of all the theatres in Sambalpur and the ticket price per show was only five rupees. The matinee show suited us all, and we joyfully discovered that each of us had five rupees to spare. So we left for the theatre. While everyone had their own bicycle, I adjusted myself on the front bar of Nandu's bicycle. After he'd pedalled half the way, we exchanged our seats.

Before leaving for the movie, I had called my neighbours from the school phone. They lived next door to our house and were the only ones who possessed a landline telephone in the vicinity. Everyone who knew about their phone used to treat them as their messengers. It probably irritated them, which was why, half the time, they didn't pass on the messages. But I made sure that they would inform my mother.

That was my first visit to a place like Laxmi Talkies, an experience still etched in my mind. It was dark inside the hall, with dilapidated seats and the coir wool coming out of the covers in places. A few men whistled, but I couldn't see them. All of us sat in the second row from the front. The dialogues echoed in the hall and it was an experience in itself to see the big heroes, the big villains and the big heroines on that screen.

Time and again, someone or other kept opening the door under the Exit display, which used to illuminate the front few rows and blur the picture. Every time in those split seconds of light, I noticed a few familiar faces in the initial rows. They were the rickshaw pullers who used to drop off a few primary-class students to our school. It felt good to see them and I mentioned them to my classmates. Sushil told me to shut up and concentrate on the movie.

'Amrish Puri will rape someone now!' he told me without looking at me, his eyes glued to the screen.

I wanted to wave at the rickshaw pullers. But they, too,

were just concentrating on the screen. So I had no choice but to resume looking at Amrish Puri. I loved the fighting scenes of the movie and the double roles of the heroes made it extremely interesting. At interval, the yellow light bulbs were turned on and doors of the theatre were opened. Suddenly, everyone got up from their seats and left the hall. I looked around to see how many people had turned up to watch the movie. They were all men, and I found that it was just the few of us who were neatly dressed. The rest of the crowd looked as if they had come from the slums.

Sushil looked at my expression and said, 'Paanch rupaye ki ticket mein yehi jugaadd milega.' [This is all you can expect for a five-rupee ticket.]

All of us ignored Sushil's comment and went to the toilet. A long queue welcomed us in front of those eight or ten urinals. I was appalled at the condition of the place. Water was leaking everywhere and the stench of urine filled my nostrils! Cigarette butts and bidis—the locally rolled cigarettes—floated in the water on the floor. There were a few dumped in the urinals as well. The red stain of paan spit had painted every nook and corner of the toilet. Most of the people took a leak first, and then went out to have a quick tea. I felt sick to my guts and could not bear to think of eating or drinking anything at that time. Had it not been for the exciting film, I would probably have left. The film was good and it made me forget the surroundings.

It started from where it had stopped, and soon we were all

absorbed in watching. The heroes were able to beat the villain in their new avatars after rebirth!

~

Dusk had fallen by the time we all came out of the movie theatre. We ate a few samosas and drank a cup of tea each from a nearby restaurant, after which my friends dropped me off at the bus stop. I was the only one who had to catch a bus to get back home. They left when I was able to find the bus that I was supposed to board.

It had been a great day for me—my first outing with my friends in Sambalpur! I was happy and excited. However, unlike other days, on that evening, I was boarding a late bus. Usually, by that time, I would be at home. This evening I expected to reach home only by dinner time.

There were only a handful of people inside the bus. Most of the seats were empty. As the first few rows were not so good for long-distance travel, I found myself a seat at the rear of the bus. It was on the right side of the aisle, next to the window. I slid open the window pane to let the fresh air in, and started to look outside.

The street lights were on and so were the lights in the small shops. Inside the bus, it was close to dark. There were lights installed on the roof of the bus, but since the insides of the lamp shades were full of dirt and dead insects, most of the light was getting blocked, creating a faint glimmer. The driver ignited the engine, and the bus started up with a vibration, followed by a creaky sound that became a part and parcel of the journey.

An old man sat diagonally behind me, towards my left. I saw him staring at me. He appeared strange. He was chewing paan. He was bald apart from a patch of hair behind his ears, and wore a thick pair of glasses. I could faintly see that he was dressed in a shirt and a dhoti. Every time I looked at him, he felt uncomfortable and tried not to make any eye contact with me.

But from the left corner of my eye, I watched him observing me. I tried to recall if I had ever seen him earlier, but I didn't recall any such moment. Soon, I decided to ignore him and tilted my head towards the window and got absorbed in looking outside. I thought about the scenes from the movie and then remembered I still had the history exam the next day. I kept thinking about a lot of things. Then tiredness took over me, and I don't recall when I fell asleep. I woke up with a start when I suddenly felt someone's hand on my shoulder. It was the conductor pulling at the collar of my shirt.

'Ticket! Ticket!' he asked when he saw me awake.

I blinked and looked here and there to make sense of where I was. I realized I had been in a deep sleep. The bus had travelled a lot of distance in this time. At present, it was halted at one of the bus stops. I looked outside to see which stop it was and found that I was halfway home. Almost everyone else from the bus had gotten down at that stop.

'Ticket! Ticket!' the conductor reminded me again in his typical style.

'Yeh lo. Aur soney do usey,' [Take this. And let him sleep] a voice from behind me said.

It was the same strange old man. In his right hand, extended towards the conductor, he held a two-rupee note. I looked at him and then at the conductor, who looked at both of us. Just out of the sleep, I couldn't make a lot of sense of this reaction from the old man. I slipped my hand in my pocket to pull out my change, but the old man stopped me.

'Nahi, nahi, Uncle. I have money.' I insisted on paying on my own.

'Don't worry, I will take it from your father. I know him,' he responded.

The conductor took the money from him and left us to go and sit next to the driver on the bonnet of the engine in the cabin area.

At the back of the bus, that old man and I were the only passengers.

'You know my father?' I inquired with a lot of interest.

'Yes.' He smiled and came to sit next to me.

I felt nice that someone knew my father and had paid my bus fare.

I squeezed in towards the window, giving him more space to sit. He made himself comfortable and put his arm over my shoulder. I kept my two-rupee note back in my pocket.

I had saved two rupees and, at the back of my mind, I was planning to treat myself to either a samosa or a jalebi from the Ram Bharose snacks shop under the huge banyan tree in the Kaccha Market.

'So where do you study?' the old man asked me.

'Guru Nanak Public School.'

'Oh, very nice, very nice!' he said.

I smiled back and turned my head to look outside.

'Come to our home tonight. There is a kid of your age in my house too. You can play with him. And my house is close to yours,' he offered politely.

'No, no, Uncle, I have to go back to my home,' I excused myself.

'You know, I have gifted him a video game. It's called Mario. Have you ever played it?' he persisted, and then pushed me back to stretch himself to the window in order to spit.

The name of the video game made me very curious. I had heard about it from a few of my classmates. I had even asked my father to buy me one, but he had refused, saying it was too expensive, as usual.

'Where is your house, Uncle?' I asked the moment he settled back in his place.

'Quite close to yours, I can drop you back to your house. You want to come?' he asked, looking straight into my eyes.

'No, Uncle. I have my history exam tomorrow,' I said sadly.

'Oh! Poor boy!' he said. Then he put his hand over my shoulder and started rubbing the back of my neck. I felt a little awkward.

'Where did you meet my father?' I asked him.

He rolled his eyes, and then said, 'Hmm . . . Beta, I met him at his office.'

Now, that was odd! My father had never worked at an office!

I clarified, 'But mere Daddy toh office mein kaam nahi karte. He is a priest at the gurdwara.'

'Oh, no . . . no,' he immediately corrected himself. 'I meant, I met him at *my* office. He'd come for some work. He is a good friend of mine.' I noticed that he stammered when he said that.

My brain registered something suspicious, but I didn't do anything about it.

As he was talking to me he slid his hand down my shirt and rubbed his palm against my back. I felt uncomfortable and looked back at him, wondering—What was he up to? I immediately tried to grab his hand and was about to ask him to stop, when, all of a sudden, he clutched me tightly. I couldn't move—not a single inch!

His eyes widened, as he stared at me. I was shit scared! I froze. I was unable to understand what he was doing to me. My head was still, only my eyes moved.

It was dark outside the bus and it was dark inside it. Without any other passenger left, there was no one who could see us. The sound of the bus and the engine had muffled every other sound.

The moment I felt his other hand on my cheek, I knew I was in trouble. I looked at him. He could probably sense the fear deep down in my eyes. When I didn't move for a while and kept staring back, the anger on his face transformed into a wicked smile. His face looked very animal-like. His mouth was all red. His teeth were soiled black. Inside his dirty mouth was his red-black tongue, and the sight of it made me shut my eyes in horror.

For the next few minutes, I was his toy. He rolled his finger around my face. Some kind of petrifying fear didn't let me revolt. I was scared of shouting. I thought, even if I shouted, the conductor was too far away to hear me. And even if he heard me, that old man would have done something to me before he arrived. He could have hit me or choked me to death. I was not in a position to think what exactly he would have done to me.

I felt vulnerable and helpless. My fear had surged to such a level that I wasn't even able to pray to God. The old man slipped his fingers inside my shirt's collar and ran them across my neck. My body shivered under his hands. I felt suffocated. My mind was losing its grip. I felt my heart beating really fast. In panic, the visuals flashed behind my closed eyes—of the dark movie theatre, of villains in the movie . . . I imagined his rough hands as they touched my body. Then I imagined how the villains had killed the two heroes in the first half of the movie. They must've felt just as helpless as me. I panted. I was running out of breath and my fear was reflected in my pleas to the man, 'Please . . . please . . . mat karo, Uncle [Don't do this, Uncle] . . . please!'

I thought of my mother the same way as I had done on the first day of school. I wanted to run to the safety of her embrace. I thought of my father. I wanted him to beat up this old man. The faces of my parents raced through my mind. In a strange way, they gave me strength. And, therefore, I kept thinking hard about them.

As the minutes passed, I came to some sort of terms with what was happening. I knew I had to open my eyes—if not right at that moment, then eventually.

Just then, I felt the old man's thumb on my lips. He rubbed my lower lip, and I was overpowered by a strong aroma of paan. His face must have been close to mine—very close. I felt he was going to do something ugly with me. I struggled to open my eyes. Something within me was changing. It must have been my fear, turning into anger. I started taking deep breaths now. I realized that every moment I was turning optimistic. I was secretly telling myself that this had to end and I needed to be strong, because my parents wanted me to be strong.

And then, a strange thing happened. The visuals in my mind changed. Scenes from the second half of the movie came flooding into my mind. The heroes whom the villain had killed in the first half had come back to life. They fought back and killed the villain. I, too, wanted to fight back and kill my villain!

The old man had just moved his hand to my pants, when I opened my eyes. The fear in them had been replaced with anger. I screamed and, in no time, pulled out the pen from my pocket, removed the cap and stabbed him on his head with it. I narrowly missed his eye. The nib of the pen made a forceful contact with his face, close to the ear.

He lost his grip over me and almost slid down from his seat. He leapt to grab the seat in front in order to stop himself from falling down. He was taken aback by my rebellion. He obviously hadn't expected me to do what I had done.

For me, there was no looking back. Some kind of madness had taken over my head. I continued to scream. With every scream, the spit from my mouth spilled out on to my lips and my chin. I was breathing heavily again. I attempted to hit him again, but he held my hands in his large palms. Then he covered my mouth tightly with his other palm and pulled me into his lap. He was obviously experienced at this game, because he had managed to overpower me. Nevertheless, I kept struggling hard to release myself from his grip. I even tried to bite his hand—that was my last resort! He managed to evade that as well.

Soon, I felt drained of all my strength. I lay back, completely spent. But my eyes were wide open and there was still hope in them.

Right then I heard a voice that revived me further.

'Yeh kya kar rahe ho!' [What are you doing!] someone shouted.

I looked ahead in the distance. It was the conductor. He leapt up on the old man and pulled him away from me. He snatched me out of his grip. At the same time, he shouted at the driver to stop the bus and turn on all the lights.

The bus came to a dead stop as the driver applied the brakes, and the three of us were propelled ahead. The conductor held my shoulder against the thrust. The alarmed old man grabbed the roof bar for support. This time, I finally saw fear in his eyes. And there was anger in mine. The driver came running to the back of the bus, unaware of what was happening. The conductor shouted at the old man and asked him to get out of the bus.

The old man attempted to explain that I was like his grandchild, and that he was only showing his affection towards me. He said that that's why he'd paid for my ticket as well. He cunningly tried to take this matter up with the driver, who was unaware of what had followed, but not with the conductor. So the conductor cut him short and asked him to leave. All this while, I kept looking at that man in rage.

When he stepped out through the front door of the bus, I slipped my hand into my pocket. I looked at him as he walked back alongside the bus. When he was close to the rear of the bus, where I sat, I took my hand out of the window and dropped a two-rupee note into the street, the ticket fare that he had paid for me. He looked at me. I shut the window pane in response and looked away. The conductor was still holding on to my shoulder.

I hadn't realized it, but I was shaking.

The driver started the bus. The conductor asked me a few questions, most of which I responded with a simple yes or no. He asked me not to worry and that he was there for me. I heard and unheard it. Inside, I was feeling a surge of emotions. As time passed by, I realized the anger within me was transforming into a sense of guilt and sorrow. It didn't matter if I should have felt that way or not, but I wasn't able to avoid it.

I looked at my watch. It was 7.45 p.m. when the bus finally stopped at the Burla bus stand. I got down and started walking towards my home. It was only when I was away from the crowd and the noise of the busy bus stand, and on the silent road to my house, that I realized I had been crying. I allowed myself to cry hard. I continued to walk, and the silent tears continued to roll down my cheeks. Through my wet eyelashes, the yellow light of the vehicles approaching me glittered. A lump kept forming in my throat and, time and again, I swallowed it.

I tried to console myself. I tried to tell myself that the old man had just touched me here and there, and nothing else had happened that I should cry for. I tried to pacify my rage with the thought that I had taken my revenge by hitting him hard on his face with my pen. But, for some reason, my own reasons felt unreasonable to me.

I walked silently along the quiet road with my schoolbag slung on my shoulder, a half-full water bottle in my hand and a thousand thoughts running through my mind. Every step I took towards home increased my worry. I was about to reach home. I wondered what I would tell my mother— How would I tell her about what had happened? It was all so disturbing.

At the same time, I was scared. *What if that old man had taken the next bus and was following me right now? What if he was hiding in that dark patch on the street approaching my house, ready to pounce?* I looked back in distress. He wasn't there. I looked here and there. He was nowhere. But he was right there in my mind. The odour of his body and the smell of his paan were there in my nostrils. I wanted to throw him out of my mind. I wanted to run away from his smell. I wanted to undo all that had happened. I wanted to clean myself and wash my body, my back, my face, everywhere he had touched me.

Struggling with my fears, I managed to reach home. The moment I opened the door of my house, my father started shouting at me: 'Kitthey siga ainni der tak?' [Where were you for so long?]

His anger startled me. I was not in a position to handle it. I avoided looking at at him and walked towards my mother, saying, 'I had called Rammi Uncle to tell you that I will be late.'

My father grabbed my hand and stopped me. 'But tu late hoya kyun?' [But why did you get this late?]

'Picture dekhan chalaa gaya si,' I replied softly, looking down and waiting for him to slap me.

Mom quickly pulled me towards her and caressed my head. She kneeled down and looked into my eyes. 'Kitthey reh gaya si? Tu theek hai? Bhukh ta nahi laggi?' [Where had you been? Are you all right? Are you hungry?]

Dad continued to shout at me. I looked at Mom. I wanted to hug her and tell her everything that had happened to me. I wanted to tell her how safe I felt when I was this close to her. But not a single word came out of my mouth. I simply kept looking at her till she took me in her arms and caressed my back. I went numb and my eyelashes were moist again.

Mom asked me why I was crying.

I told her, instead, how the exam had got cancelled. 'Mommy, exam cancel ho gaya si. So we went for a movie and I got late.'

'But what is there to cry in this?' she asked.

'Bahot bhukh lagi hai . . . Daddy gussa ho rahe hain . . .' [I am very hungry . . . Daddy is so upset with me . . .] I murmured, and held back the real reason.

Mom wanted me to promise her that I would never be late in coming home ever again. In my mind, I recalled the horrible evening when I was making that promise.

That night, I slept badly. I woke up several times, and kept tossing and turning in my bed. That old man and my experience in the bus took the shape of multiple bad dreams in the night. I remained disturbed even when I got up in the morning. As a result, I screwed up my history exam. The only date and event I remembered was what had happened the previous day. I just about managed to pass the exam.

But the impression it left stayed with me for longer than that. Now I was scared to get on to a bus—something that I had to do twice every day. I became paranoid. Every time I stepped into a bus, I would make sure that I didn't see that devil's face again among the passengers.

As time passed by and I grew older, my memories of that day started fading.

Thankfully, I never met that old man again in my life.

14

Fighting to Be There

It was the second week of December. The half-yearly exams were in the past tense now. The results were due in the future—early January. We were left with a pleasant month on our hands that had Christmas, the New Year's day and a week of winter vacation in between these two holidays.

But what made December special for me was the school's Annual Day celebration. The peon brought a notice register and English Sir read out the notice for everyone.

He announced the date of the Annual Day for that year. It was the twenty-fourth of December. He also read out the list of the various events that the teaching staff had planned for that day. There were quite a few interesting events such as theatre, dance and mime.

'Interested students can give their names to—' he spoke

out the names of the teachers-in-charge after mentioning each event.

I think about 20 per cent of our class loved the Annual Day celebration because they enjoyed participating in the various exciting and creative events. The remaining 80 per cent of the class loved it as well, but for the concept of the last period being zero period. This meant that, for about two weeks till the day of the event, all the last periods in school were cancelled. The event participants were to use this period to practise, while others were allowed to go out and play games.

The whole atmosphere in the school changed during these weeks. It was a lot of fun for everyone since studies were minimal. The Annual Day was followed by vacations, so there was a lot to look forward to as well.

I belonged to that 20 per cent of the class who got excited about the Annual Day events, and who, from Day One, start dreaming of the applause that they would get after their show on stage, in front of everyone. That was a high point in my life.

I initially wanted to opt for the bhangra event, but then, the role of being an anchor for the Annual Day turned out to be the most tempting of all. The English Sir in our class had announced that the English Ma'am from the primary school was in charge of the anchoring part of the event. Auditions were to start from the next day. But my daydreaming started from the very moment Sir made that particular announcement.

Late night, at home, I prepared for my audition. I had drafted a few lines for what I was going to say. In the morning, after taking a bath, I rehearsed my lines in front of the mirror.

'Respected chief guest, teachers and my dear friends, this evening I welcome you . . .' I started by holding a virtual mic in my hands and a towel wrapped around my waist.

Mom looked at me and asked me what I was up to. I told her not to disturb me. So she gave me sufficient time to play it out in front of the mirror.

In the zero period that day, I turned up in the computer lab room. This was the room that had been allotted for the compèring auditions. I found that my competitors were already there—five boys and four girls, all from different classes. Strangely, there was no one else from my class. All the aspirants were making full use of the free computers. Some of them were busy playing Pac-Man on the machines, while others were fiddling with the screen savers flashing on various other machines. I looked back at the door. I wanted to know if I had to compete with only those nine people, or if there were more students coming in. Thankfully, no one came. But, just to be sure, I shut the door and led myself to a vacant seat.

The next time the door opened, I couldn't help but smile.

She was yet again there in front of me—the love of my life, the primary-school English Ma'am. And soon she and I were going to talk to each other. She looked even more beautiful that day! Perhaps because she had left her hair open. It was thick and black.

'Yes, students, so you are all here for the audition?' she asked.

Everyone replied in a loud 'Yes!' There was excitement in the air. I replied after everybody had answered in unison. I wanted to stand out from the others.

'All right, so let us see what have you prepared,' she said and took her seat, right next to me.

Oh boy! Her hair smelled so good.

Her presence so close to me had made me anxious. This happened to me every time we were close. I would become so aware of her that I would go numb. I was sure I would have frozen at her mere touch! Such was the effect.

It was amazing how much I wanted her to be near me and how the same nearness paralysed me, so much so that I would find it difficult to deal with it. I found it difficult to speak. Forget about speaking out aloud, it was impossible for me to even hide the flush on my cheeks. I was always eager to present only the best of me in front of her, but, with those cold hands, chattering teeth and stammering speech, it was difficult to appear even normal.

I had already expected these sorts of things to happen to me. Hence, to be better prepared, and to handle that chill in the air-conditioned room in the presence of English Ma'am, I had already drunk enough water and also been to the bathroom. I felt fairly confident.

She looked around to see who would like to present first. Her eyes rested on me.

'Ravinder, would you want to go first?' she asked.

My name sounded so sweet on her lips! I smiled. I was on cloud nine, simply because of the fact that she had remembered my name. But I was still nervous. I rubbed my palms together in an attempt to calm down.

I took a deep breath and, when I was ready, I began. 'So ladies and gentlemen, tonight we are here to celebrate . . .'

And everyone laughed. I could not figure out why they were laughing. I looked at English Ma'am.

'Ravinder, the boy has to do the anchoring in Hindi.'

I felt like I'd got a cardiac arrest. I looked at everyone. My dream had been broken, my confidence had just been shattered. There was complete silence in the room, followed by some giggling.

'You are delivering your lines in English, which is to be done by the girl,' Ma'am clarified.

'Oh, is it?' I asked. *Now, when was this piece of news broadcast?* I thought to myself, rubbing my fingers on my forehead.

'The notice that had been circulated yesterday had this point in the end,' a girl added.

Of course, it would have been there! But how come I never noticed it? Because I hadn't listened to anything after I'd heard English Ma'am's name on that day! What an idiot I had made of myself!

The plane of my audition had crashed—dashed to the ground even before it had taken off. The feeling of not being able to make it in this round made me feel frustrated and helpless. I went back to take my seat.

The teacher called the next boy in line. He delivered a few lines. He was good with them. I hated him—not because of his good speech, but because of Ma'am's sudden interest in him and his speech.

'Very good!' she said, and then clapped. So the rest of the folks clapped too!

Except me. I wanted to be different from the others.

'What's your name?' she asked him.

Now what is there in his name? I wondered. Okay, fine, he delivered a good speech, but then asking his name was a bit unnecessary. To be honest, he wasn't exceptional. Just a little more than average. And I could have done a better job than him, if only . . . I cursed myself for not having listened properly. I cursed myself for daydreaming at the mention of Ma'am's name and not listening to anything beyond it. But what could I do now!

There he was, the star of the moment.

'Ma'am, I am Paarth,' he said softly.

I looked at his legs. I wished he would break one of them.

One by one, everyone delivered the speeches they had prepared. The boys did theirs in Hindi and the girls did theirs in English.

When the bell rang, Ma'am announced that she

would reveal the names of the selected ones in next two days.

For a stupid mistake, I felt, I had lost everything. But, then, everything was fair in love and war—and now I had another idea!

From the very next morning, I started making my case to English Ma'am. I had prepared a brand new speech, this time in Hindi. All I wanted her to do was to hear it. Initially, she did not want to listen. But, when I encountered her for the third time in the day, she promised to give me five minutes of her time.

Twice in the past, I had fallen off her expectations. So this was going to be a do-or-die situation for me. She called me to the same computer lab in the recess.

I was there on time. To my surprise, so was she. It was nice again to be so close to her, more so because, this time, there wasn't anyone to distract her interest. I had all her attention. She was there just for me! I felt special.

As I entered, the air-tight door blocked out all the sounds from the world outside and we were left in a lovely silence. Only the sound of the AC in the lab made its presence felt.

I took her permission and switched off the AC. I did not want to feel cold. There were a thousand things about her, especially at that moment, which could have bothered me. But I kept my focus on what I was there to do.

And I spoke once again . . . this time in Hindi.

No one can be unlucky for a long time. Just like it happens in our movies, no matter how difficult the start is, by the end of the movie, all the dots connect and everything falls in place. Well, this day turned out to be one such ending of a movie for me, and the beginning of the next! Unlike my previous two encounters with English Ma'am, this time I rose, from my own ashes, like a phoenix. I delivered the speech perfectly!

It was another story that, the day before, I had made the Hindi teacher from my old school in Burla write the speech for me. I had taken her some of the famous gulab jamuns from Ram Bharose, in order to gently coax the best out of her. By morning, I had mugged up the speech by heart, ready to reproduce it without a single mistake.

And I had done exactly that!

The inclusion of some heavy-duty Hindi words such as 'shrimaan', 'mahodayaa' and 'vidyaarthi' managed to have a lingering effect on her mind.

'Fabulous, Ravinder!' she gushed, clapping with joy as she stood up.

How I liked that smile on her face, and loved it more because I was the reason behind it! The next moment I felt her hand on my shoulder. *That was it!* I was about to faint. That was the best moment of my life so far.

'How did you do that?' she asked me.

'It was quite easy for me!' I showed off.

Then I asked her if I could get the boy's role to do the compèring in Hindi. She asked me to wait till she announced the result in the official notice later that day.

15

The Annual Day

It didn't take too long for my dream to come true. It happened moments before the zero period, when the peon brought a circular to our class. The teacher read it out. There were names in it of the students who were going to participate in the Annual Day.

I was one among them!

For the next two weeks, the most awaited period of the day was the zero period. There were just the three of us for compèring—Nikita from Class VIII for the English speech, I for the Hindi one and my beloved teacher!

We would meet every day. We would prepare our speeches, and then make adjustments. We would take the updated ones and see how to make the transition from the Hindi speech to English, and back to Hindi. The entire event list had to be divided between Nikita and me, so that we could focus on it better. We both were very competitive and constantly bickered if the other got the chance to take up a particular event, so we would toss a coin. Ma'am would simply laugh at our childishness, but her smile and her shining teeth were killer!

To get a better grip on the flow of compèring, all three of us would rehearse together. At times, by mistake, we would end up saying something funny or making a mistake that would make us all laugh. We felt like a family. With every passing day, I was getting addicted to English Ma'am's company. My whole purpose of going to school was reduced to interacting with her in the zero period. Everything she said was like God's words for me. Everything she asked me to do was a mission, and had to be accomplished in the best way possible.

My mornings, too, had turned beautiful. While I got ready for school, I took great pains to make sure I was neat and presentable, so that she would notice me and give me yet another beautiful smile. I would make sure that my pants were properly creased, and would get very irritated if they weren't. On reaching school, I would take a round of the primary school's prayer wing just to be able to see her and make a note of what she was wearing that day. It felt nice to catch a glimpse of her in the morning. It almost became my ritual to do so. I believed her face made my morning turn auspicious.

On the days I didn't see her, I felt like something in my day was left incomplete. One day, when I found her missing in the zero period, I ran to the class teacher's room looking for her. I was told that she was absent that day. I was sorely disappointed. After the whole day of waiting to see her, the news of her absence had left me in agony.

I also felt something that I had never felt earlier in my life. I missed her—terribly. In her absence, there seemed to be a vacuum, as if everything had lost colour and life. The computer lab appeared like a dead room without her. The whole idea of Annual Day appeared meaningless without her. My presence in that school without her appeared so unreasonable. In just six days of interaction, she had become a habit for me. I missed her smile, her talking, her face and the beautiful clothes she used to wear. When Saturday came, I could not believe that the next time I would see her would only be on Monday.

I had an awful weekend. Time—which had been running so fast for the past entire week—was now, all of a sudden, crawling. Every minute of that Sunday passed like an hour. Everything around me appeared boring, even my own parents. I didn't feel like eating, and sleep, too, was miles away from my eyes. Tinku called me to watch TV with him when he found me sitting alone in our open courtyard. I said no. He asked me the reason why I was so lost. I told him he wouldn't understand.

That lifeless weekend confirmed one thing to me. I was in

love! The better-sounding words to describe that feeling would have been 'infatuation' or 'crush', but they had not made it to my dictionary by then.

I felt like I was a different person altogether. While other boys from my class were interested in the short skirts of girls of their age in the convent school, I was dreaming of romancing my teacher! *How on earth had I become that crazy?* Guess it takes all sorts to make this world.

That Sunday night I kept tossing and turning in my bed. I was waiting for the sun to rise. I rushed through the morning routine to reach school. I was way too early, and had to sit outside the entrance gate. I kept waiting for the arrival of the school bus at the main gate. The moment that happened, I stood up. My eyes were right on the front gate of the bus. One by one, everyone got down—first the students and then the teachers.

Yes! There she was!

And, suddenly, I felt a huge wave of relief wash over me. It was as if the blood choked in my veins had begun to circulate again through my body. Her presence had fuelled life back into me.

Monday finally filled in the void that Sunday had created. The rest of the week was also full of fun.

～

Finally, it was the day we had been practising for all this while. It was the Annual Day.

I had borrowed a black suit and a red tie from Sushil for this day. English Ma'am had told me to go for that colour, while Nikita was supposed to wear a red sari. I guess she was wearing her mother's. She had told me that she was getting a new blouse, but the sari was old.

I reached the school by 4 p.m. The event was scheduled for 6. The whole school was buzzing with activity. On one hand, the stage was getting the final touches; on the other hand, there was chaos in the green room behind it. My life was much easier than many of the other participants, since I didn't need a fake beard or a bald head or any other prop. I just had to be myself. And I was all set to impress everyone in my borrowed suit and tie.

At 5.30 p.m. English Ma'am arrived, looking for both of us. I saw her from far away and ran towards the stage to impress her. She saw me running towards her. She waved at me and asked me to slow down. But how could I have slowed down! In that black suit, I felt as if I was going to take her to my prom night.

'You look dashing, Ravinder!' she said, and put her hand on my shoulder.

I looked at her hand on my body, and then at her face, and then took in the whole of her. She looked stunning in that golden-black sari. She had left her hair open. Her lips had a wet gloss and her perfume was magical. She looked taller in her heels. Her small blouse offered a nice view of her slender waist.

She was like . . . Okay, I wanted to marry her.

'Thank you, Ma'am,' I said, quite blankly, as I didn't know how to react.

'What happened?' she narrowed her eyes and asked me with a naughty smile.

'You look so beautiful, Ma'am!' I gushed.

'Oh . . . ho ho!' She laughed, gracefully holding her hand over her mouth. As she spoke, her head swung from side to side, and then right back towards me. Her hair followed her head like waves in the ocean. I swear that moment was worth capturing on camera!

'Thank you, Ravinder!' She bent forward and adjusted the knot of my tie.

I felt very important.

She asked me to follow her to the teachers' room. I asked her why. She didn't say anything, but took my hand in hers and started walking.

I was about to faint! My hand was in her hand! Was this really happening? *Oh boy!* It really was!

Beyond an iota of doubt, I can say that that moment had the potential to drive me mad or even strike me dead with an overdose of unexpected joy. I had wanted this to happen— for her to hold my hand—but the timing of it was all wrong. In the next half hour, I was supposed to be on stage, in front of everyone—the school, the teachers and the chief guest. And her sudden touch had made me forget my lines!

I lived through this adrenaline rush till we entered the teachers' room. There was no one inside. The lights were off but the leftover evening sunlight was good enough to be able to see. Ma'am let go of my hand and went to get something from her cupboard. I quickly brought my hand to my face, and, smelling it, gave it a kiss.

She turned back with something in her hands, which she didn't show me immediately. She took a chair and asked me to come up to her.

'This is for you,' she said, revealing a red silk pocket handkerchief.

I was beyond happy to see it. *She had actually thought to get me something!*

She looked into my eyes. I felt shy and blushed. She smiled and tucked the handkerchief in the pocket of my coat. Underneath that pocket, my heart was beating fast enough either to register itself in the Guinness Book or to get admitted to the local hospital.

As she was so close to me, I breathed deeply in the scent of her body. I wanted to tell her what I felt for her. But then, I hadn't prepared myself for that revelation. And, even without it, that evening was magical. I felt as if I was on top of the world! My luck was rolling and God was generous enough to make my wishes come true.

Half an hour later, I was on stage.

I looked at Ma'am sitting right in front of me in the front row. She gave me a thumbs-up sign. I looked at my pocket handkerchief and smiled at her.

The next two hours were awesome. I grew more and more confident as I spoke, and the transitions from my speeches into those of Nikita's happened very smoothly. People clapped every time we came on to the dais to close the previous event and introduce the next one.

And then, just as it had started, the evening came to an end. Nikita and I took a huge applause—another moment I would never forget.

After the event, I met up with English Ma'am near the entrance of the green room. It was where most of the performers were getting their make-up removed and changing their dresses. Even before I could say anything, Ma'am approached me. Nikita, too, was right next to me.

'Brilliant!' she said, as she congratulated the two of us. We thanked her. But Nikita left us as soon as she heard her father calling her name from a distance near the podium.

I bade her goodbye and thanked God for allowing me some private moments with English Ma'am. It was the ideal time to celebrate my newly formed bond with her. I didn't want the evening to end. I wanted to hold her hand. I wanted to feel her. I wanted to smell her.

I thought the best way to prolong that moment was to return the pocket handkerchief she'd got for me.

'Here,' I said giving that red silky square back to her.

She made a face and asked, 'Didn't you like it?'

'No, no. This is just beautiful!'

'Then keep it. I got it for you.'

I felt bubbles of love coming up inside me.

'Really?' I asked. I wanted to make sure that that handkerchief was for me, and that she had thought about me and bought it especially for me. She gave a huge smile and nodded.

Then it was time to go. It was the last day of school for that year. Ahead of us was the winter vacation. For the very first time in my life, I didn't want to take a vacation.

The realization that I would now see her only the next year was making me emotional. I wondered if she too was going to miss me. It was close to 9 p.m. when she bade me goodbye at the main gate of the school. She waved. I wished her a merry Christmas and a happy new year in advance, and waved too. But she looked at my hand, and then brought down her waving hand to shake my hand.

She left the place, and I left only when she was out of sight.

I had discovered my first love at the age of fifteen!

That night I couldn't sleep.

I began making a new year's greetings card for her.

It is the second day of January—a brand new year. My body smells of Pears soap and my face smells of the Ponds cold cream that Mom has forcibly rubbed on to it, and which otherwise I avoid. I wear the red school sweater over my uniform.

I am excited to return to school. It has been exactly eight days now since I have seen English Ma'am. I am finally going to meet her today. I cannot suppress the smile that's playing hide-and-seek on my face.

All through my journey from Burla, I prepare for what I will say the moment I see her. In the crowded bus, perched on to the bonnet adjacent to the gear stick, next to the driver's seat, I am lost in my own thoughts. The noise of people, the squabbling of two ladies at the back over who had grabbed a seat first, the loud monetary negotiation between the conductor and a passenger—it all fails to make its way to me. My mind is relaxed and fresh. There is joy in my heart. Everything around me looks beautiful, even the helper of the bus who appears as though he hasn't taken a bath in a week.

Every time the bus driver applies the brakes, I skid a bit further on my perch. The impact jerks me back to reality, reminding me of the thing in my hands, which I must keep absolutely safe.

It's a greetings card that I had made on a folded white chart paper. It's too big for my schoolbag, so I am carrying it in my hands.

'I have to give it to someone special in my school,' I tell the driver when he asks me what it is. I tell him to drive slowly, so that it does not get soiled. He smiles at me.

I have painted it with watercolours. There is some cotton stuck on the paper to replicate winter snow, even though I've never seen snow in my life. I think the snow is romantic. There is also a picture of the red silk pocket handkerchief in it. I know she will recognize it. It is our secret.

From the bus stop till my school, I walk, guarding the card with utmost care. A mad truck speeds past me and splutters dirt on to me. In that cloud of dust, I have stepped into a puddle and spoiled my shoes and socks. But I am happy enough to have managed to save that card.

By the time I reach the school gate, I am tired of holding that card, but I hope she will love it. I've been holding it that way for more than an hour and a half. I keep the card on my desk and clean myself up. I want to look perfect when she sees me for the first time after the long break.

In every corridor of the school, everyone is wishing everyone else a happy new year. I don't stop to wish anyone; nor do I respond to their wishes. I creep, then walk and then run to the teachers' room. I want to give her my wishes before anyone else does.

Minutes before the students and the teachers assemble for the prayer, I am in front of the teachers' room. A number of teachers are gathered around the long table in the room. They are all busy wishing each other. I knock at the door to ask for permission to come in, but in that loud crowd, no one can hear my knock.

Unable to stop myself, I slowly walk in.

Right then, something strange happens—I notice that the teachers are not quite wishing each other. They are all saying congratulations to a particular someone. There are laddoos in their hands.

I hear her name. And I hear it again.

I feel a tap on my shoulder. It is our Punjabi Ma'am. Before she can ask me what I am doing there, the Hindi Sir calls out from the other corner of the room, 'Arey, Punjabi Ma'am, suna aapne? Hamaari English Ma'am ki shaadi tay ho gayi hai. Aaiye, muh meetha kijiye!' [Have you heard the news! Our English Ma'am's marriage has been fixed. Come, have some sweets!]

I hear that, loud and crystal clear.

All of a sudden, I can no longer move. I feel a deep pain in my chest, as if someone has stabbed me. I can't hear any voices any more. In front my eyes, there are teachers, so many of them, but I fail to identify them. They ask me what has happened. I don't answer them. I stand there with my greetings card in my hand.

I try to move my feet, but I have once again frozen. I try hard to move. I don't want to cry in front of everyone. All of a sudden, I hear her voice. But I no longer want to face English Ma'am.

I run away from that place.

16

In Sadness and Defeat

From being someone who followed the English Ma'am everywhere she went, I now became the one who tried to avoid her at every step. From someone who waited the whole day to get a glance of her, I actually started hiding from her. Whenever I saw her walking down the corridor towards me, I would turn around and hide somewhere. Once or twice she even called out to me, but I didn't listen. How could I? I felt cheated by her. I also felt a deep sadness within me.

My friends asked me the reason for my gloominess, but I didn't say anything. I just shook my head. I began to avoid my friends and sat alone even during the break. Then, one day, while I was sitting on a bench outside the field, Nikita walked up to me.

'Hi,' she said with a smile.

I didn't respond, but my sad eyes probably told her the story.

'Listen, I know you like English Ma'am,' she said hesitatingly.

I was shocked. *How had she come to know? Could she just figure out! Was I that transparent?*

But I chose not to admit it.

'What? What are you saying?' I asked with as much surprise as I could manage.

Girls are probably more mature than boys—at least, Nikita was.

'It's okay. My mother says it's normal for us to have infatuations at this age. This is a sign of our growing up . . .' she was going on, but I wasn't listening.

All I was thinking was if Nikita was able to find this out, soon my friends would find out too. Or, seeing me here with Nikita, they would think I was getting attracted to her! There would be no end to their teasing me.

Nikita was still talking.

'Nikita . . . I . . . I . . . have to go, I have a class,' I blurted out, and ran away from her.

From then, I tried to act as normal as possible. Studies came to my rescue and I began to think only about my subjects and how I would do well in them. I began working hard for my board exams. Soon I began to feel normal again.

The day I heard English Ma'am had got married and quit the school, I didn't feel quite as much pain.

~

I thought my board exams for Class X had gone off quite well. I kept saying so to my parents, who were always worried. There was still some time before the results would be announced. Everybody was tense about it.

So far, in my entire school life, I had been in the top 10 per cent of my class. It didn't matter how fun-loving I was; I had managed to stay near the top ranks. But, in all these years of school, I was yet to achieve my ultimate goal of topping the exams. There were about a hundred students in the same class at Guru Nanak Public School, divided into several sections. Being the topper at this school was not an easy thing.

With all my hard work, I had managed to secure the second rank in the half-yearly exams of Class IX, which had again dropped to the third by Class X. But I had a lot of expectations from the board exams that I had written.

When the results came out in June–July, I was in for a shock. I had scored 69 per cent in all! This was the first time I had ever dropped below 70 per cent!

The topper from our town had scored 75 per cent. I was 6 per cent behind him. In the '90s, anything above 70 per cent was a great score and a reason to celebrate. Mothers whose kids had done well had all the reason to call up and flaunt their kids' marks in front of those whose kids had scored less.

'My son scored 72 per cent. How much did yours score?'
As if you didn't know?

I felt ashamed, embarrassed, guilty and humiliated, all at the same time. It had been my worst performance ever. And the board exams are discussed beyond the boundaries of school—across towns and cities. It's a benchmark, I guess, for the entire nation. I had hopelessly slipped up on this benchmark.

When you expect fewer marks, you are able to handle this situation better. But when you expect to excel and something of this sort happens, you first have to learn how to come to terms with the dashing of your own hopes, and then cope with everyone else's opinion about it. It was now that phase of my life.

At first, I went into denial. I sent in my papers for rechecking. But there was no luck. In Hindi, I had still scored 41 out of 100. My proficiency in the national language had pulled my entire percentage down. Some of my close friends tried to console me by saying that I should be happy because I had scored 98 out of 100 in maths. But they knew, as well as I did, that maths couldn't change my aggregate.

As the reality of the low marks sunk in, I slowly went into a state of depression. The mothers of the batchmates who had scored better than me kept running into my mother and haunting my life. I wanted to run away to someplace else, where no one asked me about my exams or expected anything else of me. I wasn't good enough for those expectations and those expectations weren't good for me. Instead of treating my friends as friends, those expectations had made me start viewing them as my competitors. This should not have been the case.

Besides, despite all my hard work, I had scored way less than expected. What else could I have done?

I decided to give up.

One day, I broke down in front of my mother and told her that she or my father should not expect anything great out of me, because I wasn't as good as everyone else. I was smart enough but not the best, and I felt suffocated in this madness to become Number One.

Mom wiped away my tears. She made me lie down with my head on her lap, and stroked my forehead affectionately. She told me why she wanted me to succeed. She told me how my father worked hard to afford all the expenses of my education. She told me that my father hadn't been able to complete his own education, because my grandfather hadn't been able to afford it. Perhaps that's why Dad made it a point that I took my education seriously.

Mom told me about the sacrifices that both of them had been making, only to afford a good education for my brother and me. She never asked Dad for new clothes for herself—only for us. She never did any shopping for herself, only for us. As a family, we never went out to a restaurant for a meal—we always ate at home. Before she told me, I never knew that most of the money that my father earned was being spent on our education. But it was in our hands to do the rest.

She told me that getting good marks for me should not be a matter of winning the rat race or showing off to everyone else. But a good education was our only way of bringing the family out of poverty. Our parents were not even concerned about themselves, only about my brother's life and mine. The only way for us to have a good life when we grew up was to score the finest of results.

Whatever Mom said that evening kept ringing in my head for a long time. She had her reasons and, indeed, she was right in holding them.

As the days passed, I even started liking the song *Papa kehte hain*. It had started making a different sense to me. Soon, I wanted to become the one who could sing that song and prove to the world that I meant every word of what I was singing.

This time, there was a positive change within me. I no longer envied those who were ahead of me in the rat race. I felt calm, composed and focused solely on my own goals. And then, just like that, I returned to the rat race . . .

But this time, I no longer felt like a rat.

17

Grand Finale to School

Class XI started on a brand new note. I opted for the science stream. I promised myself that I would beat everyone else in my class. I now clearly knew what my goal was. And I had planned an entire strategy to achieve it. But then, there came an obstacle—a giant 6′ 1″ of it—and placed itself right in between my goal and me.

He had a name as well—Nitin Ramchandani. A Sindhi who hailed from my own town, Burla, and had recently joined my school in Class XI, Nitin had one half-blackened tooth and a dark patch, almost half an inch in size, underneath his left jaw. Every time you looked at him, he would give you an unnecessary smile.

He had studied till Class X at St Joseph's Convent School (yes, the one where girls wore skirts!) and had come to Guru

Nanak Public School because the convent didn't have Classes XI–XII, something I too would have had to do had I gone to that school.

In the initial days we used to treat him and all the other new entrants like step-classmates, if such a term can exist. It was not a nice thing to do, but it was our way of venting our frustration at not having the privilege of studying at the convent. *Why had they had all the fun?*

However, I was not at all jealous. I was happy that there was finally someone in my class who was from my hometown. In the past three years, I'd not known anyone in Burla to whom I could reach out and discuss homework, or sit with and prepare for examinations. It was quite natural, then, that Nitin and I formed a good bonding in the very first month. By the second month, we had visited each other's houses and had eaten meals cooked by each other's mothers. That made us best friends—so we were! And the last-minute preparations for a unit test, the late-night revisions at his place and other such things had made us grow even closer.

But the results of the unit test made me realize how wrong I was. That giant, with his half-black tooth, had grabbed the top rank in my class!

I had come second.

I could not believe it. I had beaten the old top-rank holders but had lost the battle to this grinning monster!

There is no pain more brutal than to see your good friend get ahead of you in the race that means a lot to you. From that day onwards, I started envying Nitin. His only crime was that he had scored better than me.

On his face I congratulated him. But behind his back, I started bad-mouthing him.

'Itna lamba hai, phir bhi basketball nahi khelta—what a waste of height! He should have been playing basketball!' I kept saying, until it became a matter of public embarrassment for him.

Just like other students from the convent school, he was good at English. He was also extremely good at biology. At times, even the Bio Ma'am would forget the scientific names of some of the organisms from the animal kingdom, but Nitin would remember. Not only that, he would, at times, correct the teacher when she ended up making an unconscious mistake.

'No Ma'am, the scientific name of the chimpanzee is *Pan troglodytes*. Hominoidea is for apes,' he once corrected the teacher.

'Lagta hai zoo mein kaam karta hai!' [Seems like he works at the zoo] I immediately quipped, and everyone laughed. But Nitin laughed along with them, and that shut me up. I had wanted him to feel embarrassed. But, hell—it seemed like he didn't even know the emotion!

~

There is no substitute to jealousy. No matter how many times I went over to Nitin's place to study with him, I would still envy him for being a better student than me. I hated it when our common friends in class approached *him*, instead of me, to solve their problems. It was part of his practice to read a chapter the day before it was supposed to be taught in the class. So he had an answer for every question, and soon became the apple of every teacher's eye. He was somewhat weak in maths, so he made a smart move to compensate—he started taking tuitions from the schoolteacher early in the mornings.

Nitin's grey Chetak scooter was another reason for my jealousy. While I would go to his house on my bicycle, he would come to mine on his scooter. He was rich and, on weekends, used to ride a green Mahindra jeep with his leg out on the stepper. I only liked his scooter when he used to offer me the rear seat and take me for a ride to the Burla market.

There was a huge difference in Nitin's and my unit test marks, despite the fact that I had doubled my efforts, and started praying as well. I no longer prayed to God for getting me good marks. Instead, as per my new strategy, I would pray to God to limit Nitin's score.

Nitin, again, was one of those irritating people who just before the exam would say, 'Phatt rahi hai meri. Bus, Bhagwaan, is subject mein passing marks aa jayein.' [I'm in a terrible shape. Please, God, let me at least score passing marks in this subject.]

'Amen!' I would say in front of him, but would silently add to his prayer, 'Please, God, hold him at the passing marks only.'

'Sardaar, kyun chidta rehta hai tu mere se! Chal, aa, exam dete hain,' [Sardar, why do you seem so upset with me! Come, let's go and give the exam] he would say, dismissing the whole issue.

On the top of it, my mother and father loved Nitin. They found him sincere as well as easy-going. They would let me go to Sambalpur or other distant places late in the night, if only I went with Nitin. My father knew Nitin's father well. There were only a handful of people in Burla who were highly respected in the society, and Nitin's father was one of them. I loved his parents as well. Even before I knew Nitin, I knew his father—every summer, when we used to pluck jamuns from our jamun tree, Dad would ask me to take a basket to Nitin's house. In return, Uncle would give me a packet of biscuits or a chocolate.

If only his son would have scored a little less than me, the two of us would have been best friends. But destiny had its own plans.

The next unit test went by. I slipped to the fourth place this time, while Nitin successfully stayed at the top. Slowly, half a year and a few more unit tests passed by, but nothing changed this pattern. The only change was that now, instead of just our class, the entire school knew Nitin. He became the head boy of the school. He came, he conquered and he ruled, in a school that was *mine* first, and only then his! It was his habit to agree with everything that the teachers said. If they said yes to something, Nitin would nod his head first, and only later think about what they had said. And when they said no to anything, he too would shake his head. Once I saw him agreeing to two opposite opinions over the same issue with two different schoolteachers. He was good at marketing. The product he marketed well was himself.

'How can a boy like you, from a different school, become the head boy in this school?' I asked him in frustration one night.

Nitin was very forthcoming and honest. He explained things to me that no one had taught me at school. He told me what to do and not to do in order to hold influence. He gave me some quick tips to get people's attention. He was good at it.

Taking a chance, I implemented his lessons, and soon I became a house captain. I realized that it wasn't such a big deal—just a little bit of tact, awareness and a play of words, and 75 per cent of the work was done. With this sense of achievement, my attitude towards Nitin also changed. He didn't feel like a rival any more. Rather I began to respect his wisdom and sincerity towards me.

With that, in the last few days of Class XII, my hostility towards Nitin also went down. Just like it happens with a months-old new year's resolution, the importance of becoming a topper in my class also became less. It was pointless to bang my head against the strong-willed wall called Nitin Ramchandani.

For the first time, I was very comfortable and relaxed during my exams. I had forgiven Nitin for his crime of being better than me. Actually, I was too tired of being jealous. I became more carefree, and that reduced the pressure I used to face while studying. I had again begun to enjoy games, and I did play some of them with Nitin, especially after the Class XII exams were over. What was more, I loved the change!

Nitin and I developed a great friendship during the vacation after Class XII.

~

I am nervous.

Finally that moment has arrived which each one of us has been waiting for. I know I have done well this time. But what if history repeats itself? Memories from what had happened almost two years back keep flashing in my mind.

The honking of a scooter temporarily interrupts my fearful thoughts. And then I hear him shouting, 'Sardaar, jaldi aa ja!' [Sardar, come here quickly!] Nitin is bang on time.

I tell Mom that Nitin has come to pick me up. I touch her feet and run out of the house. She shouts after me, 'All the best and have faith in God!'

Outside the gate of my house, I see Nitin on his scooter. He too looks anxious. The two of us exchange smiles.

'*Chal, chal, jaldi kick maar, bhai!*' [*Hey, kick-start the scooter quickly!*] I say to him and hop on to the back seat.

The scooter springs to life and, in no time, we are on the highway from Burla to Sambalpur. We talk, but we don't know what exactly we are talking about. We are talking just for the heck of it; just to make each other comfortable.

With every mile towards the school, our nervousness starts making its way to our faces. The enthusiastic smiles vanish and a familiar fear creeps in and makes its home between the lines of our foreheads. We know we are moments away from witnessing something that can either lead us to happiness or to sorrow. I am sure about Nitin. But I am only hopeful about my own self.

At the entrance of the school, we park the scooter. We are the early birds—there is no one yet out there. Still, we race between us to reach the entrance gallery of the school. The noticeboard in the corridor is our destination.

We make a hard stop at the gallery. Our bodies come to rest, but we continue to breathe hard. In no time, we make ourselves busy trying to spot the freshly clipped A4-sized paper on the board. There are so many of them! The last-minute flurry has muddled our minds. We are no longer calm or relaxed.

'*Here!*' Nitin finally shouts, pointing to the noticeboard behind me.

His words make time stop for a moment. I turn towards him and feel an adrenaline rush. I can almost hear my heartbeat now.

I read: '*Rank-wise Class XII (Higher Secondary Examination) CBSE Results*'. I am seconds away from seeing how I have done.

Nitin points his finger to the first row. I don't follow his finger too carefully, knowing that he will top the school, as usual. I don't want to waste my time congratulating him, as long as I'm fighting my own fear and trying to know my fate.

My eyes scroll down to the second row. I don't see my name. The typing is terrible on the result sheet. I look down to number three, and then number four. In my hurry, all I am trying to look for is the initial letter 'R'. I don't see it.

My fear is again coming true. Oh God! I am not there in the top ten rows. I am about to break down. I am shouting that I don't see my name! I am calling out to Nitin and telling him that I don't see my name.

He grabs me by my shoulder. He is trying to tell me something, but I am not listening to him. I continue to shout aloud.

He slaps me hard.

I'm stunned. I ask him if he can find my name.

'You arsehole! What else am I doing?' he shouts at me, and then points his finger again to the first row.

I finally look at where his finger rests on the board. I read the first alphabet. It is 'R'. I read the rest of the name. It's me.

Oh God! It's me! I take my time to understand what that means, and to come to terms with the reality.

'Sardaar! Fattey chakte tu taan!' [Sardar! You've made it!] Nitin screams out, and gives me a tight hug.

Oh boy! I have finally made it! Yes! Yes! Yesssssssssssssss!

I AM THE TOPPER. I–I–I–I–I–I–I—AMMMMM— THE—TOPPPPERRRRRR!

It is an unbelievable moment for me. I can't express how I am feeling. I keep staring at the noticeboard. There are a thousand things I want to do. But, for the time being, I want to run to my parents. I want to tell them that I have come first in the school! Finally.

Epilogue

I scored 76 per cent in my Class XII exams, and there wasn't anyone in the entire Burla and Sambalpur who could level my score. For some reason, Nitin scored less than what everyone had expected of him. His rank had dropped by not one but three spots! Both he and I knew that he deserved a lot more than what he had got. He was the real topper, in a sense. He had been an outstanding student for the past two years. I was convinced that one board exam could not justify someone's actual merit. The good thing was that Nitin was disappointed only for a few weeks. After that, he moved on.

I took admission at Guru Nanak Dev Engineering College in Bidar, Karnataka. Once again, just like it had been when I had moved from my old school in Burla to GNPS in Sambalpur, I was the only one in my class at college to have come from Orissa to Karnataka. Back then, there was a Sikh quota in that college, and with my grades I had managed to get a seat in Computer Science without having to pay any donation. They called it a free seat. Once again I was separated from my old friends, all of whom had stayed back in Orissa. I knew things were going to change, but what remained unbroken by this distance was the bond of friendship between Nitin and me.

As of today, Nitin is the Country Head (Sales and Marketing) of a construction equipment multinational in India. I think it is the perfect job for the boy who could influence teachers and become the head boy of a school in the very first year of his joining! Only last year, he got married to Anu. The two of them live in Pune. Nitin and I continue to meet at least once every six months, when we recall the old times and share a laugh.

My younger brother, Jitender aka Tinku, has been in the United States for the past few years. While he followed my footsteps in every step of life—from the first school in Burla to the next school in Sambalpur, the engineering college in Bidar and landing up a job in Infosys—there is one thing in which he managed to overtake me. He got married before me. My NRI brother visits us once every year. The last time he was in India was for the occasion of my wedding.

Then, surprisingly, one day I found Sushil on Facebook! We relived the good old days online, until, when I was in Kolkata for a day, he visited me at the hotel where I was staying. In those couple of hours that we spent together, we took a trip all the way back to our past—to the schooldays and beyond. We also updated each other on what the others from our class were doing now. It felt good to know that everyone had settled down well in life.

While I have moved from Orissa to Chandigarh in search of my destiny, my father still believes that Orissa is his 'karma bhoomi'. Despite Punjab being his birthplace—where his roots are—and despite my willingness to move to North India, my father finds it difficult to leave Orissa. For him, it's a place where he has worked hard for more than thirty years, and where he has seen his children growing up. As I complete this book now, I also want to say sorry to Dad for hating him at times through the years—the time when he took me to school for the very first time, or each time he took me to get those injections. I cannot imagine what my life would have been today, had he not done all those difficult things!

My mother spends half of the year with me, and the other half with my father back in Orissa. This is her way of sharing her love with both of us. I love to see her smiling, because I am aware of the sacrifices she had made, for years, for my brother and me. If she wouldn't have given up everything for us and our education, we certainly would not have been what we are today. I'd like to thank her with all my heart for it.

And what's my status?

Well, I have picked up the profession of storytelling and I am enjoying it thoroughly. By the time you read this line, I would have started writing yet another story . . .

Acknowledgements

I would like to thank my wife Khushboo for always being with me on the journey of writing this story; and for throwing some very interesting thoughts at me each time I was stopped by writer's block. How we laughed together when you narrated the story of your schooldays in the capital city of Delhi, and I picked up topics to relate to them from my own schooldays in the remote town of Burla!

I give my sincere thanks to Vaishali Mathur, Senior Commissioning Editor at Penguin Books India, for always standing by my side to take care of my work and improve it further; and for all the patience she invested in awaiting the chapters from my side. And yes, you are super fast with all your work on my books. Indeed, without you, this dream book would not have been possible.

I would also like to thank my editor Monidipa Mondal for jumping into the chaos of my world of work and finding some of the brilliant logical mistakes. I hope someday we would reveal those mistakes as part of 'the making of this book'.